SUNSHINE AT HOME

AND

OTHER STORIES.

SUNSHINE AT HOME

AND

OTHER STORIES

By

TIMOTHY SHAY ARTHUR

American Fiction Reprint Series

BOOKS FOR LIBRARIES PRESS

FREEPORT, NEW YORK

1970

First published in 1864
(Item #129; Wright's AMERICAN FICTION 1851-1875)

Reprinted 1970 in *American Fiction Reprint Series*
from the edition of 1866

INTERNATIONAL STANDARD BOOK NUMBER:
0-8369-7021-7

LIBRARY OF CONGRESS CATALOG CARD NUMBER:
74-137722

PRINTED IN THE UNITED STATES OF AMERICA

ARTHUR'S
HOME
STORIES
NEW YORK.
SHELDON & CO.
RICHARDSON SC. N.Y.

SUNSHINE AT HOME

AND

OTHER STORIES.

BY T. S. ARTHUR.

NEW YORK:
SHELDON & COMPANY, PUBLISHERS,
498 & 500 BROADWAY.

1866.

C. A. ALVORD, STEREOTYPER

LIST OF SERIES.

I. *HIDDEN WINGS, AND OTHER STORIES.*

II. *SOWING THE WIND, AND OTHER STORIES.*

III. *SUNSHINE AT HOME, AND OTHER STORIES.*

CONTENTS.

SUNSHINE AT HOME,

AND OTHER STORIES.

I.

SUNSHINE AT HOME.

SUNSHINE for home plants is just as necessary as sunshine for garden plants ; yet from how many homes is the sunshine banished! It is no wonder that so many children grow up morally blanched, or with strange, one-sided developments of character.

Without heart-sunshine, beaming from radiant faces at home, the affections cannot blossom in a fragrant promise of good fruit. The proposition being self-evident, needs no enforcing argument. Thought assents. But a picture from real life, may give the precept an active force in some heart which otherwise might continue to dwell in the darkness of its own sickly fancies, instead of coming into the sunlight.

"But how," asks one, "am I to get sunshine into my home?"

"Open the doors and windows," we answer. "The heavens are full of warm light. Open the doors and windows, and it will come in."

"How am I to open the doors and windows? It is easy to say open them! But how?—how?"

We will undertake your case, friend. It is a difficult one, we own; your doors and windows have been shut so long, that bolts and hinges are rusty. Lichen and moss have grown over a hundred narrow chinks where single rays used to penetrate; and close-leaved ivies are hanging their curtains in front of old loop-holes through which, at least once a day, in former times, the sun glanced in to two or three small chambers of your guarded dwelling. Your children, the home-plants whose culture has been so unwisely neglected, are sickly and deformed in their moral growth. They do not adorn, and beautify, and make vocal with all sweet melodies, your home. There is small hope for them, unless you open the doors and windows of which we have spoken, and get them into the sunshine.

It is evening, and you have turned your feet homewards. What have you been doing all day? Gathering in and hoarding what you have already lost the power of enjoying. Is it not so? Let your thought go away down into consciousness. Look at the face of your real self. How is it? Do you, in any true sense, enjoy the good things of this life, which you are spending your life to obtain? You enjoy, if the word may be used, the excitement of getting; but, in the dispensation of your gains, how little of true pleasure is evolved!

And so, when you turn yourself away from your counting room, and look homeward, the shadows begin to fall around you, and you bring these, instead of sunlight, into your dwelling.

They are falling around you now. The feet that bear you onward, are not winged by sweet anticipations; but seem heavy-laden. You have left all light heart-pulses behind you. It is with you now as it has been for months; we might say, years. You know how it will be on your arrival; and how it will not be. No throbbing of glad little feet down the stairs and along the hall will answer, like musical responses, to your first steps, long waited for. And yet there are young feet and children's voices in your dwelling. Thus it will not be. But, instead, the sharp notes of wrangling, or the dissonant cries of passion, are the sounds that wait for your reluctant ears. The memory of what has been is too distinct in your mind for any thing like self-forgetfulness. The shadows fall more and more heavily around you; there lies a weight upon your bosom. Expecting the worst, you are going home prepared for the worst.

But this is not well. Try if you cannot take home with you a little sunshine. It will be such a novel thing, that we should not wonder at any magical results which might follow.

"It is easy for you to say, Take it home.

But where am I to find the sunshine of which you speak?"

You are not very anxious to get home, so turn aside with us into the public square by which we are passing. You rarely go through it, I believe. There is plenty of heart-sunshine in there about this hour of the day. Maybe a ray or two may find a path through the cloud that envelops you, and brighten you with its radiance.

What a pleasant transition from the hard, red pavement, and the stiff, red houses! We pass, in a moment, from city to country. From the unlovely aspects of trade, to the graceful beauty of a sylvan scene. The tall trees shut us in from brick and mortar; and we look down the vistas and winding avenues, upon soft, green lawns; and the plash and murmur of the fountains are in our ears. Let us sit down, just here. The low declining sun shines slantwise through the cloud of spray, and a rainbow is seen faintly above it, resting there like a crown. How rhythmical that sound of falling water!

It does not come to the ears in a monotonous flow, but cadenced, like music. Is not the scene beautiful and tranquillizing? Do you not already perceive its influence in a calmer tone of feeling? Now look at that rosary of children, singing gleefully as they dance around one of their number, a blue-eyed, golden-haired, fairy little thing. Let us sit down here. It will do you good, I am sure. Yes, it is already doing you good. The dull indifference of your eyes is passing off. We see a new expression coming into them. Happy children are like flowers, they delight us with beauty and fragrance.

Here comes a sweet little cherub. She has left her companions, and her feet are bringing her this way. You have held out your hand for her, and she sits, now, upon your knee—sits and looks up into your face, and asks you childish questions, that you find it pleasant to answer. Your hand lies amid her sunny curls; you gaze into her face half wonderingly; the old father-feeling stirs in your heart, and if its impulse were obeyed, you would hug that little one tightly to your bosom.

A voice calls the child; a hand is reached out for her; you take a kiss from her cherry lips, and now she goes dancing away. But she has opened a window in your heart, and a few sunbeams went streaming in among the dust and cobwebs. Don't shut it again too suddenly. Let it stand open for a little while, so that you may get an impression of their pleasant warmth.

How happy are all these children! How kind and loving! Your ears have not once been jarred by an angry voice. A father passes, holding by the hand a little boy and girl, just the ages of two children in your home. They are talking to each other and to him in the happiest frame of mind, and he is entering into all that they say with as much apparent earnestness as if he were no older than they. Now they have stopped at only a few paces away from us. What has happened? There is a difference of will in the two children, and both show persistence. The boy wishes to take one curving road to a gate, and the girl another.

"Well, what is to be done?"

The father does not speak impatiently, but with a calm gravity that must subdue, rather than excite the children.

"I want to go this way," says one.

"And I want to go this way," said the other.

"We can't go both ways at once, that is certain, unless we cut ourselves in two, and let the right sides go to the right, and the left sides go to the left."

There is a grave humor in the father's voice and manner as he says this. Both the children laugh merrily.

Now you would have said, had the case been yours, and said it in a way to banish all kind feelings from their hearts, "I don't want any wrangling about which way you will go. One way is just as good as another. Come!"

And away you would have swept, at a quickened pace, making for the first gateway, and disregarding all appeals to let them stay longer. But this father is more careful than you in respect to the sunshine. He will not suffer it to be withdrawn, if possible—no, not for a moment. He has great faith in sunbeams. You would have been annoyed and angry. You would have punished them for disagreement. You would have said, in your thought, "If they cannot appreciate the beauty and pleasantness around them, they shall not have the privilege of its enjoyment;" and, acting from this state of feeling, you would have shut up the bitterness in their hearts, and let it rankle there.

"We can't go both ways at once." The father stands still, patiently waiting for the children to agree upon the path they will take. His mock-grave proposition has amused them, and they do not lose temper.

"Let father choose," says the little girl.

"Yes, let father choose." The boy is pleased at the suggestion.

"Then I take another path—that one down where the squirrels are at play."

And off they go, with the sunshine even brighter about them than before.

You have at home as beautiful a child as the golden-haired one who sat on your knee a little while ago, and a boy and a girl just the ages of the two whose laughing voices, as they went by in harmony just now, is still a pleasant sound in your ears. Have you ever come with them to this place? The question half surprises you. Of course not. You have graver matters requiring attention.

Graver? Think about that. Is not the life more than meat, and the body than raiment? What are these graver matters? Oh, they are included in the word business. They appertain to the meat and the raiment. You are building up, in toil and self-denial, a fortune for your children, taking thought for nothing but their great material interests. But is the splendid edifice you are erecting for them to be a temple or a tomb? Open, on all sides, to the sunshine of gladness, or windowless as a mausoleum? What are the good things of earth to him who has no faculty of enjoyment? Sir, cultivate the faculty of enjoying life in your children, if you would secure their happiness in the future. Let in the sunshine of a tender, wise, loving heart upon them. Take home with you, this very day, a thoughtful, cheerful, self-possessed spirit, and let that meet, undisturbed, the disturbing life which has so long made life discordant there. It rests with you, Sir, to change the quality of things in your household. To make your children loving and forbearing among themselves, and obedient, from affection to their parents. It is the sunshine that they want, and moral beauty and health are impossible without it.

You see the whole subject in clearer light. Your heart feels warmer and more cheerful. You will carry home a sunbeam, if possible.

Well, you are at your own door. You feel a shadow already in the air. Your state of mind is changing. But don't, we pray you, weakly yield to the pressure of old states. Break up this bad habit. Think now, and act from true thoughts; let judgment bear sway over feeling. Force a smile to your lips, and kind words to your tongue. If there is discord, seek to remove the cause; but do not throw the fuel of passion on the flames.

The door is shut behind you. How quiet all seems! There is something ominous in the brooding stillness. You move along the hall, wondering at the silence. Whispering voices are now heard.

"There is father!"

The tone involves a threat of unhappy consequences. There is something wrong. You begin to close the windows through which sunshine was streaming. Open them again quickly. There.

Now you are in the household room. Eyes look at you strangely, and then turn to John, your oldest boy, who sits with a pale, troubled face. He has done wrong in something, and is waiting for the burst of your anger, and the punishment that you mete out occasionally with angry severity. He does not expect *you* to come in sunshine ; he looks only for a storm.

"In trouble, John?" How kindly you did say the words ; and see what a sudden light has come into his shadowed face.

"Yes, sir."

He says it in a tone that disarms you, for it expresses sorrow and hope in your forgiveness.

Well, what is it, my son !"

Still you are kind—so kind *for you!*

"I know you will be angry, father——" He pauses.

"Perhaps not, my son."

Was it really you that spoke? How strangely all eyes look upon you.

"You can't help being angry ; it was so wrong in me. But indeed, father, I was not thinking. I don't know what came over me ; and I have been so sorry. Maybe I can save enough by Christmas to buy a new one."

"A new what, my son? Don't be afraid to tell me. I shall not be angry. If you are sorry for a wrong act, I will let repentance make all right between us again."

How wonderfully you are controlling yourself! All this is a new experience for you, and as new for the members of your household. They look on you with a light of surprise and inquiry in their faces.

John comes forward and stands close to you. He has taken your hand—he has leaned his head against you—he cannot look up when he owns his fault. You start. There is an angry throb in your pulses. No—you had not expected that! John felt the start—and he guesses too well at the anger in your bosom. He still holds your passive hand, but does not dare to press it, for fear the movement should cause you to throw it away. Oh, strive hard now for the mastery over yourself! Do not lose the vantage ground you possess. Do not shut the window through which sunlight has begun to stream. Do not drive away in anger the boy who has approached you in sorrow and repentance.

"John!" He lifts his eyes to yours instantly, and you see that they are full of tears. "The fault is serious, but I am sure it was not wilfully done."

"Oh, no, no, father, it was not wilful, but accidental."

"And you are forgiven, of course."

Did you really smile benignantly as you said that? It must have been so; for a light seemed to fall over every face around you.

Think, now, how different it might have been if you had come home in your usual cloudy temper. If no sunbeams had broken through to thaw love's frozen fountains. Now you have gained a power over that boy's wayward heart for good, which, if you will but retain it, may influence all his after life. You have gained, also, a power in your home. There will be, for this time, a readier obedience to your word; a new regard for your comfort and wishes; a more cheerful spirit with all. And it will be your own fault if the influence now gained become not permanent.

Have we answered your question as to how the windows and doors were to be opened, so that sunshine might enter your dwelling? If you tell us nay, then we fear your case is hopeless. The doors and windows of your own heart must first be opened, remember. The sunshine must come first into your own darkened chambers, or we see no promise of light for the shadowed chambers of your home.

II.

THOUGHT FOR THE MORROW.

OF the many passages of the Divine Word which come down to our common life, in their plainest literal signification, there is none, the wisdom of which we find oftener demonstrated than this: "Take no thought for the morrow. Let the morrow take thought for the things of itself. Sufficient unto the day is the evil thereof." And yet, we are always taking troubled thought about to-morrow; and always proving its folly.

By way of illustration, let us consider the case of our neighbor Cartwright, over the way—a very common one. He is in business, and, like too many in our time, has used the credit system a little too freely, both as to taking and giving. The consequence is, that in regard to money-matters, things do not always glide on smoothly. When notes are given, the due day is certain to come are given, the due day is certain to come around, and payment may not be deferred without loss of credit, and, in most cases, ruin. It often happens that these notes mature long before the goods, for the purchase of which they were given, are sold and paid for; and where the actual capital is much below the range of business done, a great deal of anxious "financiering" has often to be encountered.

You have the case of our neighbor Cartwright in a nut-shell. And now, let us consider this case from a closer point of view. Let us come into our neighbor Cartwright's individual consciousness, and see how it is with him in his daily life.

It was three o'clock. The banks had closed their doors, and the credit of all who had paid their notes was safe. Mr. Cartwright sat quietly at his desk, with a pleasant sense of relief in his mind, though rather wearied as to the body. He had passed through what is known in business phrase as a "hard day." How he was to get through was more than he could see, when he arose in the morning. In fact, he had been awake for more than half the previous night, taking anxious thought for the morrow, planning, scheming, worrying, and had risen with a headache, in consequence, which kept him faithful company up to the moment when the last hundred dollars, needed to complete his payments, came into his hands. It is to be noticed that this wakeful planning and scheming, when he should have been asleep, availed him nothing; for, of the various ways and means that were suggested to him, not one proved of any value on the next day. The day's efforts developed the day's resources. So his anxious thought for the morrow, hindered instead of helping, by robbing him of the strength he needed for the day's duties when they came.

"It is surprising how things come out!" said Mr. Cartwright as he sat musing at his desk. "I didn't see the way at all clear in the morning; yet, it opened before me, first on this side and then on that, in a most unexpected manner; and here I am, all safe again. Well, well!' What's the use of this worrying one's self to death? I had my night of trouble all for nothing."

Even while Mr. Cartwright was saying this, his hand had reached out for his bill-book, as a thought about to-morrow's payments intruded itself.

"Let me see how much is to be provided for," came audibly from his lips, as he laid the book open before him. For the next three or four minutes he made figures on a small piece of paper rapidly.

"Three thousand four hundred dollars!" he murmured at last, in a half-surprised, half-desponding tone. "Three thousand four hundred dollars!" he repeated; and then sat very still for more than a minute.

"I don't see the way clear at all!" And he shut the bill-book and returned it to its place. "Where is this large aggregate to come from? Well, well, well! One day's trouble is scarcely over before the next day's trouble begins. Three thousand four hundred dollars to provide for, and not one hundred in bank!"

Mr. Cartwright was in no mood for home-enjoyments when he returned to his family, as the evening shadows came down. His little Eddy sprang into his arms, hugged and kissed him with childish eagerness, and said, in his earnest, loving way:

"Dear papa! I'm so glad you have come!"

Yet, even while the father held his sweet boy in his arms and drew him to his heart, the thought of to-morrow's cares came in to mar his happiness. Why did he not push this thought aside? Why did he not say to the evil spirit of distrust, "Avaunt!" Habits are strong. They may well be called a second nature! And of all bad habits, distrust is one of the most inveterate, because oftenest indulged. It had become a habit of his mind to ponder anxiously on the future, and he could not rise above it now.

His wife's smiling welcome home came next. She had his soft slippers, dressing-gown, and easy-chair ready. She knew that his day's duties were hard upon him; and, therefore, she sought to make the hour of his return an hour of comfort and pleasure. Mr. Cartwright felt now, as always, the sweetness of that love which pervaded the atmosphere of home like a fragrant incense, and sighed for lack of power to enjoy it fully.

"Isn't your tea right?" They were at the table, and Mr. Cartwright had his cup to his lips. Just as he placed it there, a shadow fell over his face. But there was nothing wrong in the tea. A thought of the morrow had come in like a death's-head to his feast.

"Three thousand four hundred dollars." No, it wasn't the tea.

"Nothing could be finer." And he pushed back the intruding thought, and forced a smile to his countenance.

"Don't you feel well?" Mrs. Cartwright was not entirely satisfied. She saw that her husband's smile played but lightly on the surface.

"A trifling headache; that's all." Mr.

Cartwright knew that signs of care were in his face, and that he could not wholly obliterate them by any mental effort. So, he said "a trifling headache."

It was true as to the headache. That was, however, but trifling, as he said, and would hardly have been noticed, but for want of an excuse for not looking cheerful. His wife talked in her pleasant, interested way, of the day's incidents; of the persons she had seen; the social news she had heard; but failed to keep his attention. While she talked on, he was thinking of to-morrow, and pondering the ways and means of getting his notes out of bank.

"I don't believe you've heard a word I've been saying!" said Mrs Cartwright, pausing in her talk, and looking a trifle annoyed.

"Indeed, you're mistaken!" replied Mr. Cartwright. "I've been listening to every sentence. Go on."

"If so, what was I talking about?"

Now, this was pressing him too closely.

"Why, about——"

Mr. Cartwright stopped and looked a little confused.

"I knew it!" broke in his wife, with her face of a warmer tone. "So, if you feel no interest in what I am saying, I will keep silent."

Her manner was slightly offended.

"Forgive me, dear," said Mr. Cartwright. "A thought about to-morrow came into my mind, and I could not push it aside."

"What about to-morrow?" asked Mrs. Cartwright, her manner changing.

"Oh, a mere thought of business."

"Business! Why don't you leave business at the store?"

"I try to do so, but am not always successful. Care is a most insidious intruder, and will come stealing in at times when he is most unwelcome."

The light faded from Mrs. Cartwright's face. She loved her husband, and could not feel happy if she knew that his mind was in any way burdened. And now silence came down upon them; and they sat to the conclusion of their evening meal with scarcely the utterance of another word.

After supper, Eddy tried to get up a romp with his father, but Mr. Cartwright, whose current of thought was setting strongly in the direction of to-morrow, pushed him aside after a little while, saying—

"Papa's head aches to-night, darling."

The child moved away with an instantly sobered face; and Mr. Cartwright, with shut eyes, and a look of care on his countenance, leaned his head back against his easy chair, and sat without speaking again for nearly an hour. Then, in very shame for such weakness, he aroused himself, and made an effort to talk cheerfully with his wife. But the conversation was too forced to be of long continuance. There was a weight on the feelings of Mr. Cartwright which depressed both tone and manner, and silence soon came down again.

And thus it was, that troubled thoughts of to-morrow came in to rob the present of its peace.

"Take no thought for the morrow," said Mr. Cartwright to himself, with an effort to withdraw his mind from a state of anxious brooding over the burdens of the day to come. It was nearly midnight, and all in the household but himself were in the calm forgetfulness of sleep. "There is no use in all this. It but robs me of strength to do to-morrow's work."

But like a bow that is bent, his mind flew back instantly, to the state from which he had tried to withdraw it, and kept on searching about for the ways and means of compassing to-morrow's payments. A dozen different schemes were thought of; a dozen modes of procedure conned over; but no solution of the difficulty was presented.

At last, wearied nature gave way, and about two o'clock in the morning, he lost himself in the dreamy mazes of a troubled sleep. Thought had been too highly stimulated for repose, and so kept on without the equipoise of reason. Mr. Cartwright was still among his account-books; and still busy in the work of money-raising. At five o'clock he awoke in a state of wild disturbance, frightened at the apparition of a notary. When fairly in his senses, his lips parted with an ejaculation of thankfulness that it was only a dream.

Mr. Cartwright did not sleep again. He was nervous and exhausted as he appeared at the breakfast table, and took his morning meal in almost total silence.

"You are not well," said his wife anxiously.

"Not very," he replied, "I slept indifferently last night."

"Does your head ache still?"

"Yes."

"Badly?"

"No; but badly enough to put my nerves in a flutter. The fresh air will make me feel better, I hope."

"What is to be done?" was the anxious question that Mr. Cartwright asked of himself, as he passed from his dwelling, and took his way to the store. A number of suggestions had come to his mind in the anxious night-watches; and two or three of them had been favored as dernier resorts in case help came not from other and more desirable sources. This was all the aid his troubled pondering had brought him.

The morning letters were on Mr. Cartwright's desk. He sat down, and looked at them with a kind of faint hope that they contained remittances. One, post-marked St. Louis, he opened first. He had a customer there who had been written to for settlement of his accounts; and this might contain a draft. He broke the seal nervously. Yes! A remittance! No! only a note of twelve months to close the account. Mr. Cartwright felt as if some one had struck him. Twelve months! In a half indifferent way, another letter was opened. It contained a draft! His hands trembled as they unfolded the narrow strip of paper. "Five hundred dollars!" He could hardly believe his eyes. He read again. Yes, it was true. The amount was from an old customer.

"So far, so good!" came almost cheerfully from his lips, under a sudden reaction of feeling. Another seal was broken, and there was another draft; another seal, and another remittance; until over sixteen hundred dollars lay smiling before his eyes. He still sat, with the morning's letters before him, only half read, when a customer came in to settle an account. Three hundred dollars more were added to the day's receipts; thus giving him, with his small balance in bank, about two thousand dollars towards the thirty-four hundred, the magnitude of which had so troubled him.

By twelve o'clock, Mr. Cartwright was "made up," and his notes out of bank. But not a single dollar had come through the ways and means he had planned in so much anxiety through half the sleepless night. Worry had not brought him a single pennyworth of help. He had robbed his family of their evening's pleasure, and all for nothing.

"What folly!" he said to himself, as he

thought over these things, seated at his desk, in the comfortable state of mind that succeeds the accomplishment of a dreaded day's payments. "Why should we take such anxious thought for the morrow? It does no good; for things never come out as we plan them. For all the help it brings us, we might let thinking and planning alone, from set of sun to daylight."

As he closed the sentence, Mr. Cartwright thought of to morrow's burdens, and took down his bill-book, to determine their magnitude.

The shadow came over him again, for they were almost as heavy as the burdens of today had been. Would they be laid off as easily? He had no well assured hope of this. The ways and means were not visible. And so he went home again, at nightfall, with the old pressure of care on his heart, and the old, disheartening concern about tomorrow.

III.

THE CLERK'S MARRIAGE.

"You are a brave young man, or a very foolish one!"

"Why do you say that?"

"To think of marriage."

"What has bravery or folly to do in the case?"

"The young lady is poor."

"I do not wed for money."

"There would be some hope for you if she were the possessor of twenty or thirty thousand dollars. But being as poor as yourself, the folly of this purpose stands out in bold relief. Look before you leap, my friend; there's trouble for you on the other side."

"I am not sordid, Mr. Blair." The young man's fine face glowed, and his eyes flashed with a repressed indignation.

"Not sordid enough, Adrian, for marriage, as society is now constiituted. There are two sides to this question of marriage; the sentimental side and the matter-of-fact side. Now, you have looked only at the sentimental side. Suppose we consider the matter-of-fact aspects. You are a clerk, receiving a salary of one thousand dollars. How much have you saved?"

"Nothing to speak of."

"Nothing! So much the worse. If it costs you a thousand dollars per annum to live, from whence is to come the means of supporting a wife and family?"

"Oh, I've been careless and wasteful in expenditures as most young men are. I had only myself to provide for, and was self-indulgent. But that will cease, of course."

"Granted, for argument sake. The young lady you propose to marry is named Rosa Newell."

"Yes."

"A charming young girl; well educated; finely accomplished; used to good society, as we say; and just suited for my friend Adrian, if she had money, or he had an income of three or four thousand a year. But the idea of making her a happy wife, in the city of New York, on a thousand dollars, is simply preposterous. It can't be done, sir; and the attempt will prove ruinous to the happiness of both parties to so foolish an arrangement. It is a matter of the easiest demonstration, Adrian; and I wonder so good an accountant as you are, should not, ere this, have tried this question by mathematical rules. Let me do it for you. And, first, we will look at Rosa's present sphere of life. She has a home with Mr. Hart, an uncle, and is living in rather a luxurious way. Mr. Hart is a man who thinks a great deal of appearances, and maintains a domestic establishment that does not cost less than four thousand dollars a year. His house rent is equal to your whole salary. Now, in taking Rosa from this home, into what kind of a one can you place her?"

A sober hue of thought came over the young man's face.

"You cannot afford to rent a house at even

one-half the cost of Mr. Hart's, even if you were able to buy furniture," continued Mr. Blair.

"We shall board, of course," said Adrian. "Housekeeping is not to be thought of in the beginning.

"If not in the beginning, how afterwards?"

The young man looked a trifle bewildered, but did not answer.

"What are you now paying for board?"

"Five dollars a week."

"You would require a parlor and bedroom after marriage?"

"Yes."

"At a cost of not less than fifteen dollars a week."

Adrian sighed.

"We could hardly afford the parlor."

"Hardly," said his friend. "Well, we give up the parlor, and take a pleasant front chamber on the second floor, at twelve dollars a week. But the house is not first class, nor the location very desirable. These are not to be had in New York at twelve dollars a week. You cannot afford for Rosa the ele gancies of her present home. Three dollars more a week for washing and et ceteras, and your income is drawn upon at the rate of seven hundred and eighty dollars a year. Two hundred and twenty left for clothing and all other expenses! And, so far, it has taken nearly three times that sum to meet your own demands. It has a bad look, Adrian."

"I was wasteful and self-indulgent," replied the young man, in a voice from which the confident tone had departed. "It will scarcely cost Rosa and me for clothing one-half of what I expended."

"Say one-half, and your income will not reach the demand. What was your tailor's bill last year?"

"One hundred and sixty dollars."

"Say two hundred, including boots, hats, et cetera?"

"Yes."

"You could hardly get this below a hundred and fifty."

"Perhaps not."

The young man's voice was growing husky.

"That will leave seventy dollars for your wife's clothing, and nothing for pleasures, recreations, little luxuries, or unanticipated but unavoidable expenses. And if it be so with you two in good health, what will be the condition of things in sickness, and with children to support and educate. Adrian, my young friend, there is debt, embarrassment, disappointment, and a miserable life before you. Pause and retrace your steps before it is too late. If you love Rosa, spare her from this impending fate. Leave her in her pleasant home, or to grace that of a man better able than you are to provide her with the external blessings of life. You cannot marry on a thousand dollars a year, and it is folly to think of it."

"We could get boarding for ten dollars a week," said Adrian.

"That would scarcely help the matter at all. At best, it would only make a difference in the amount of your indebtedness at the close of each year. It is folly to think of it, my young friend. You can't afford to marry."

"It has a dark look, but there is no holding up now," replied Adrian, in a gloomy way. "We have mutually pledged each other, and the day of our marriage has been appointed."

"I'm sorry for you," said the friend, a bachelor of forty, who, on an income of fifteen hundred dollars a year, could see no possible chance for a happy marriage in the city of New York, and preferred celibacy to the embarrassments which he saw hundreds of his friends encounter in their attempts to live in a style out of all proportion to their resources. "I'm sorry for you," he repeated; "but if you will bend your neck to the yoke, you must not complain of the burden you find yourself compelled to bear."

Strange as it may appear, the young clerk, Henry Adrian, had never before looked this matter of income, expenditure, and style of living, fairly in the front. The actual aspect of the case, when clearly seen, threw his mind into a state of troubled bewilderment. He went over and over again the calculations suggested by Mr. Blair, a book-keeper in the establishment where he was employed, cutting off a little from one proposed expenditure and another, but not being able to get the cost of living down to the range of his salary, except when the style was so far below that in which his wife must move, that he turned half sick from its contemplation. The more steadily he looked at the truth, the more heavily came the pressure of its stony weight upon his heart. To go forward was little less than madness, yet how could he hold back now?

Rosa sat alone, reading, in one of her uncle's handsome parlors, waiting for her lover. He was later than usual; so late that her book began to lose its interest, and at last lay closed on her lap, while a shade fell over her expectant face. A single glance at Rosa's countenance revealed the fact that she was a girl of some character. There was no soft, voluptuous languor about her, but an erectness of position as she sat, and a firmness of tone in all her features, that indicated an active mind, and self-reliance.

An hour later than usual, Adrian came.

"Are you sick, Henry?" asked Rosa, as she took his hand, and fixed her eyes on his sober face.

"Not sick, but troubled in mind," he replied without evasion.

"Why are you troubled, Henry?" And Rosa drew an arm tenderly around her lover.

"Sit down, and I will tell you. The trouble concerns us both, Rosa."

The young girl's face grew pale. They sat down close together, holding each other's hands. But in Adrian's countenance there was a resolute expression, such as we see in the countenance of a man who has settled a question of difficult solution.

"The day fixed for our marriage is only two months distant," he said. The tone in which he spoke chilled the heart of Rosa.

She did not answer, but kept her gaze on his face.

"Rosa, we must reconsider this matter. We have acted without forethought."

Her face became paler, her lips fell apart, her eyes had a frightened expression.

"I love you, Rosa, tenderly, truly. My heart is not turning from you. I would hasten, rather than retard, the day of our marriage. But there are considerations beyond that day, which have presented themselves, and demand sober consideration. In a word, Rosa, I cannot afford to marry. My income will not justify the step."

The frightened look went out of Rosa's eyes.

"It was wrong in me ever to have sought your love."

Her hand tightened on his, and she shrank closer to his side.

"I am a clerk, with only a thousand dollars of income, and I do not see much beyond to hope for. Rosa, the furniture of these parlors cost twice the amount of my salary. The rent of the home in which you now live is equal to what I receive in a year. I cannot take you from all this elegance into a third-class boarding-house, the best my means will provide. No, no, Rosa, it would be unjust, selfish, wrong, cruel. How blind in me ever to have thought of so degrading the one I love!"

The young man was strongly agitated.

"And this is all that troubles you, Henry?"

"Is it not enough? Can I look at the two alternatives that present themselves, and not grow heart-sick? If we marry, what is before us? Humiliation, deprivation, and all the ills that poverty brings for you, and debt, trouble, and a lifelong embarrassment for me. If we separate, each taking different ways in life—oh, Rosa, Rosa, I am not strong enough to choose that alternative!"

And his form trembled under the pressure of excitement.

"You love me, Henry." The voice of Rosa was calm, yet burdened with feeling.

"As my own life, darling! Have I not said so a hundred times?"

"And even as my life do I love you, Henry."

For several moments her face lay hidden in his bosom. Then lifting it, Rosa said—

"I am glad you have spoken on this subject, Henry. I could not approach it myself, but, now that we have it before us, let it be well considered. Your income is one thousand dollars?"

"Yes."

"A sum large enough to supply the real wants of two persons who have independence enough not to be enslaved by a mere love of appearances."

"Why, darling, it will require more than half of my salary to pay for respectable boarding."

"Taking it for granted that, after our marriage, I am to sit down in a boarding-house, with hands folded, an idle dependent on your labor. But I shall not so construe my relation to my husband. I will be a helpmeet for him. I will stand by his side, sharing life's burdens."

"All this is in your heart, darling, I know," returned Adrian. "But we are hedged round by social forms that act as a hindrance. You cannot help me. Society will demand of us a certain style of living, and we must conform to it, or be pushed aside from all circles of refinement, taste and intelligence. I cannot accept this ostracism for you, Rosa. It is not right."

"As if a false, heartless world were more to me than a true, loving husband! Henry, the central point of social happiness is home; as the home is, so will our lives be—rather let me say, as we are, so will our homes be—centres of gloom or brightness. What others think of us is really of little account in making up the sum of our enjoyments as we pass through life; but what we are in ourselves is every thing. We must be the centres of our own world of happiness, or our lives will be incomplete. Can a fine establishment like this, in which I live in weak dependence, fill the measure of my desire? Can it bring peace and contentment? No, no, Henry. The humblest apartments, shared with you, would be a palace to my soul instead. I am not speaking with the romantic enthusiasm of an ardent girl, but soberly, truthfully, Henry. No, dearest, we will not make our lives wretched by living apart, because we cannot make a fair appearance in other people's eyes. God has given us love for each other, and the means of happiness if we will use them. Let us take his good gifts in thankfulness. You have an income of one thousand dollars. We must not expect to live as those do who have two, or three, or four thousand dollars a year. Be that folly far from us, Henry! I am equal to the self-denial it will require, if the word 'self-denial' is to be used. Are not you also? Oh, Henry! is there any joy to be imagined beyond that which flows from the conjunction of two loving hearts? and shall pride and a weak spirit of social conformity come in to rob us of our blessing?"

The young man had come, sternly resolved

to put off the day of marriage. He parted from his betrothed that night, looking forward with golden-hued hopes for its arrival. They had talked over the future, practically and sensibly. The lover's fond pride, which had looked to a fair social appearance for his young wife, gave place to a better view of things. He saw that his love had fixed itself upon a true woman, and that in the humbler sphere in which their lot was cast all attainable happiness was in store for them, if they would but open their hearts in an orderly way for its reception. One thing said to him by Rosa in that evening's talk we repeat, for the sake of young wives, or maidens on the eve of marriage.

"Be mine, dear Henry," she said, "the task of ordering and regulating our domestic affairs in conformity with your means. I will give all thought to that. Your income is fixed, and I shall know exactly the range of expenditure we must adopt. Do not fear debt and embarrassment. These wretched forms shall never enter your home, while I stand sentinel at the door. If the husband gives his life to care and work, shall not the wife do the same? If he provides to the best of his ability, shall not she dispense with wise frugality his earning? She that fails to do this, is not worthy of her position."

"And so you are bent on this folly?" said the bachelor clerk, on the day preceding that on which Adrian was to be married.

"Yes, if you choose to call it folly," was the answer.

"Where are you going? To Saratoga?"

"We shall go nowhere."

"What! not make a bridal tour?"

"No. A clerk who only receives a salary of one thousand dollars can't afford to spend a hundred in making a bridal tour."

Mr. Blair shrugged his shoulders, and arched his eyebrows, as much as to say: "If I couldn't afford a bridal tour, I'd not marry."

On the day after Adrian's wedding, he was at his usual place in the counting-room. He received from his fellow clerks a few feeble congratulations. Most of them thought him a fool to burden himself with a wife not worth a dollar.

"When I marry I'll better my condition; not make it worse," was the unspoken thought of more than one.

"Where are you boarding?" asked Mr. Blair, indifferently, two or three weeks after Adrian's marriage.

"Nowhere," was replied. "We are at housekeeping."

"What!"

"At housekeeping."

"What is your rent?"

"Two hundred dollars, and half of that my wise, good little wife is to pay in music lessons to our landlady's daughter. We have two pleasant rooms in a third story. I furnished these with the money it would have taken for the usual bridal tour. Rosa has the use of the kitchen, and insists on doing her own cooking and housework for the present. I demurred, and do demur; but she says that 'work is worship,' if performed conscientiously and dutifully as she is performing it. And, with all this, we are very happy, Mr. Blair, as you shall witness. To-morrow you must go home with me, take tea and spend the evening."

Mr. Blair accepted the invitation. He had met Rosa, occasionally, before her marriage, and knew her to be a bright, accomplished young woman, fitted to move in refined and intelligent circles, and he felt some curiosity to see her in her new position of mistress and maid to her own household. The Third Avenue cars bore the two men a long, long way from the city's throbbing heart, out to the more quiet exteriors where they alighted, and after a short walk, entered a modest looking house with well tended shrubbery in the little front garden. To the third story they ascended, and there the young wife met them. Not blushing and with stammering apologies for their poor home; but with such ease and self-possession—with such a happy light in her eyes, and such loving smiles about her lips—that Mr. Blair felt himself all at once transferred to an earthly paradise. As soon as time came for observation, he took note of what was around him.

The furniture of the room into which he had been ushered, could scarcely have been plainer. In the centre, stood a small breakfast table, covered with a snowy cloth, and set for three persons. Four cane-seat chairs, a work stand, a hanging shelf for books, a mantel ornament or two of no special value, an ingrain carpet on the floor, and plain white curtains looped back with blue ribbons, made up the complete inventory. No, not the complete inventory; for there was a piano against the wall; the dark case and plain style of which showed it to be no recent purchase. The instrument had been Rosa's, as the observant visitor correctly inferred.

After a pleasant talk of some minutes, Rosa left the room, and not long after returned, bearing a tray on which were tea, toast, butter, biscuit, cold tongue and sweetmeats. There was a beautiful glow on her face as she entered, but nothing of shame or hurt pride. With her own fair hands she arranged the table, and then took her place at the head, to serve her husband and his friend.

The heart of Mr. Blair glowed and stirred with a new impulse as he looked into the pure, sweet, happy face of the young wife, as she poured the tea, and served the meal which she had prepared.

After supper, Rosa removed the tea things, and was absent nearly half an hour. She returned through her chamber, which adjoined their little parlor, breakfast and sitting room, all in one, with just the slightest change in her attire, and looking as fresh, happy and beautiful, as if entering a drawing room filled with company. The evening passed in reading, music, and pleasant conversation. As Mr. Blair was about retiring, Adrian said:

"Do you think, now, that we were fools to marry?"

Rosa stood with her hand drawn within one arm of her husband, and clasped; and with a face radiantly happy.

The Young Married Clerk and his Bachelor Friend.

A shade crept over Mr. Blair's countenance.

"No, not fools, but wise, as others might be, if they were only courageous enough to do as you have done. Mrs. Adrian," and he took the young wife's hand, "I honor your bravery, your independence, your true love that cannot be overshadowed by worldliness, that mildew of the heart, that blight on our social life. You are a thousand times happier in your dutiful seclusion, than any fashion-loving wife, or slave to external appearance, can ever be."

"I love my husband, and I live for him." Rosa leaned closer to the manly form by her side. "I understood, when we married, that he was a life-toiler; that our home would be established and sustained by the work of his hands; and I understood as well that I was not his superior, but only his equal, and that if it was right and honorable for him to work, it could be no less right and honorable for me. Was I to sit idle, and have a servant to wait on me, when his was a lot of toil? No—no—no! I had my part to perform as well as he, and I am performing it to the best of my ability."

"You are a true woman, a wise woman, a good woman," said Mr. Blair, with ardor; "and you will be as happy as you deserve to be. I thought Henry a fool to marry on a thousand dollars, and told him so. But I take back my words. If such women as you were plentiful, we could all marry, and find our salaries ample. Good-night, and may God bless you!"

And the bachelor clerk, who could not afford to marry on fifteen hundred dollars a year, went to his lonely home—lonely, though peopled thickly—and sitting down in his desolate chamber, dreamed over the sweet picture of domestic felicity he had seen, and sighed for a like sweet hiding-place from the world, and all its false protection and heartless show.

IV.

NOT HAPPY—AND WHY.

No, he was not happy.

And of course there existed a reason why Mr. Leslie Holbrook was not happy. Conditions of mind are not accidental; they are dependent on causes that may be clearly traced.

The cause did not lie in any deficiency as to this world's goods. No; nor in any lack of luxuries, or home-comforts. His domestic establishment was complete; or rather establishments—for Mr. Leslie Holbrook had a country house as well as a city house; and taste and wealth had combined to enrich them with both internal and external beauty.

Time was when only one establishment existed—the city house, and that was nothing very ambitious; but, for home joy and home comfort, it gave ample dwelling place

—for these are guests easily satisfied. Their life rests not in any thing merely external.

Nothing very ambitious, we said. But as wealth came flowing in upon Mr. Holbrook, he grew ambitious to let some of his neighbors see the golden fringe on the outer mantle of his prosperity. To this a certain feeling of unrest impelled him. Mere possession gave not the inward satisfaction promised. He had made haste to get rich, because, in manhood's early spring-time, gold seemed the greatest good. "To be *rich* is to be happy"—so he translated the aphorism.

But, in his case, as in that of others, wealth did not bring happiness. It must be used as a means to happiness. That was something learned in the right direction; but, as *he* learned it, it could scarcely be called the alphabet of true wisdom. Using wealth as a means of happiness, was a different thing in his mind, from what it is in the mind of a philanthropist.

"I will build me an elegant house," said Mr. Holbrook, and the purpose gave his laboring heart an easier motion. Then thought grew busy in this direction--pleasantly busy. He consulted an architect; looked at plans; examined locations; discussed materials, style, and arrangement of rooms. How interested his mind became. How full of pleasant exhilaration. His first idea of a house gradually lost its attractions. He must have something more costly and imposing than that.

"When I build, people will expect to see something handsome." So said Mr. Holbrook; and in saying it, he gave people more credit for interest in him than was legitimately their due.

Mr. Holbrook built his fine house. Its exterior was architecturally imposing and beautiful; its interior, the very perfection of order, elegance, and convenience. But the leading end, in his mind, through all the interesting progress of this edifice towards completion, was a mean and unworthy one; and just in the degree that a man's end, in any work, is mean and unworthy, will be the degree of his failure to realize happiness in its attainment. Home comfort had, in almost every case, been a secondary thing in the mind of Mr. Holbrook. He was building a house more with the end of securing public commendation than domestic felicity.

This being so, it is not surprising that, in the actual possession of his palace-home, he failed to reach the anticipated delight towards which his mind had been reaching. In a little while his eyes ceased to range over frescoed ceilings, picture-hung walls, rich furniture and carpets. Spacious as were the apartments, his thought went soaring beyond them. Almost innumerable as were the articles of taste and luxury gathered within the walls of his dwelling, they failed of more than a passing interest. He found himself sighing amid his splendors; sighing for something only dimly shadowed in his thought—its very dimness giving the impression of a good unattainable. To this, a positive element of disquietude was added. The three days' wonder created by his architectural achievement had already passed; and his fine house was being dwarfed by the erection of another in the square opposite, so far beyond his in cost and imposing elegance of design, that eyes once admiringly turned to his palace-home, must now only see its inferiority to the other.

In the new dwelling place of Mr. Holbrook, no higher domestic happiness than existed in the old one was found. Nay, if the truth must be told, happiness had decreased inversely to the increasing splendors. This was not because of any law inherent in the case. The family of Mr. Holbrook might have been happier in their new home than they had ever been in their old one. But the elements of their happiness would have been grounded in a very different soil from love of self and the world.

The unrest of Mr. Holbrook's mind impelled it to search for some new source of interest. Mere money-getting and money-hoarding had ceased to meet the demands of his nature. He could not sit down, and find a soul-satisfying pleasure in counting his gold. He must use it as a power to wrest happiness from the elements around him.

Next in order came his country house, and nearly three years of time were expended in the erection of this, and the laying out of gardens, walks, and lawns, the planting of trees and shrubbery, the building of hothouses and graperies. But when all was finished, and the interest and excitement attendant on the thought, planning, and working involved, had died away, he sat down in the Eden his hand had created, and did not find in it the Eden of his imagination. It was perfect as a garden of beauty and delight, but its perfection did not fill his soul with interior joy. For him there was a trailing serpent among its flowery parterres.

No, Mr. Holbrook was not happy. We said so in the beginning, and repeat it here. He had gathered for enjoyment vastly beyond what it is possible for any man to enjoy alone, and still he was stretching out his hands, and drawing in more, seeking therein for the soul-delights that ever flit as deceptive marsh tapers before the selfish and worldly-minded. Business cares oppressed him ; trade brought many anxieties ; fear of loss troubled his peace at times, and drove sleep from his pillow. Town house and country house had failed as investments that were to yield certain happiness. He dwelt in one during the winter, and in the other during the summer. In the winter, looking away from the disquiet of the present, he pictured the rural delights of the coming season of blossom and fruitage, and in the restless summer, his eyes turned back to his city home as most desirable. And so the years came and went, but happiness lay still in the distant future.

Mr. Holbrook was like a hand, or an eye, or an arm, which morbidly endeavors to appropriate to its own use alone the blood that flows in from the common heart for the common good. Congestion and inflammation were the consequence. He was oppressed and feverish. He received all the freely giving arteries brought, but obstructed every panting vein, and sought to keep in his small individual organism the life blood designed for the sustenance of many.

As in the human body, so in the larger body of human society, this attempt of any member to use, *for his own good alone*, a larger share of vital blood than health requires, is always attended by pain and disability. The blood, struggling with impediments, passes onward by the impelling force that quickens instead of retarding its strokes, and completes, steadily, its circles of life, but completes them in as steadily increasing pain to the obstructing member. It cannot wholly obstruct, except in death to itself. The normal social law is as unchanging as the normal physical law. No man who lives for himself alone can be happy. It is just as impossible for an eye or a hand, endeavoring to see for itself alone, or to work for itself alone, to be in health.

So Mr. Holbrook had proved in an experience of over thirty years of mere selfish appropriation; and now, at fifty-five, with all the external good that wealth can give, we find him unhappy. Not unhappy *because* he is rich. No ; a man may be rich, and yet know as much of human bliss as comes to the lot of mortals. But he is unhappy, as hundreds and hundreds of thousands are unhappy, simply because he has cared for no one outside of the narrow circle of his home ; and never used his wealth or influence, except in a reluctant, compulsory way, in any generous efforts to serve the common good. He has grown plethoric. In vain the absorbent system strives to ap propriate the teeming richness of the too abundant blood. Their power has, long ago, been overtasked. They cannot do their work.

And so, at fifty-five, Mr. Holbrook, rich and envied—people envy in a very blind way —found that life, on his plan, was looking very much like a failure. Gold, once dazzling his eyes as the greatest good in life, palatial elegance, honor among men,—all these were in his possession, and yet the phantom, Happiness, smiled on him more faintly than ever, and flitted further in the shadowy distance.

An old school-friend came to visit Mr. Holbrook in his beautiful country home in the flush of a luxuriant summer, when his acres of lawn and garden were green with the softest grassy velvet, and starry with a thousand-hued blossoms; an old school-friend, whose life had not been so successful in the common acceptation of the word, but more successful in its higher and truer signification. He had tried to look upon man as his fellow; to regard himself as a part of society, with duties and responsibilities; and thus regarding himself, he had been a dispenser of benefits as well as a receiver thereof—proving, in many sweet instances, that it is more blessed to give than to receive.

"All this does not make you happy," he said to Mr. Holbrook, on the day after his arrival, speaking with the frankness of an old and warmly-welcomed friend.

"Happy!" returned Mr. Holbrook, his very tone repelling the words. "There's no such thing as happiness. It's a deluding phantom."

But his friend answered, in quiet tones:

"A man may be happy in this life."

"I doubt it," replied Mr. Holbrook. "Wealth does not bring it, that is certain. Rich men are no happier than poor men. It is not, then, the condition that brings the peace, tranquillity, and satisfaction we sigh for. Ah, my friend, it is a sad thing for a man at fifty-five—a man who has aimed high in the world, and hit his mark besides—to discover that something is wrong in his calculations; that the grand result he sought to reach does not include happiness. Alas! that it is so. And if I read my neighbors aright, the parallelism of our experience is complete. Yes, there is something wrong. What is it, my friend?"

And Mr. Holbrook looked at his old schoolfellow with the earnestness of a man who sought an answer to his question.

"All unhappiness," replied the friend, "comes from some violation of the inherent law of our being. Society is only a man in the larger form, and in it there is a correspondence to even our very physical constitution. Assuming this as the groundwork of illustration in attempting to reach an answer to your question, I take this piece of twine and tie it around your finger below the second joint. Now we have a violation of the law governing the circulation of blood, and a serious obstruction is the consequence. Your finger holds a larger supply of the rich juices that feed the toiling members than it can possibly appropriate to any use, and so swells and grows purple with congestion. Now, as the engorgement increases, pain is felt—pain not only in the finger, but along the arm; and should the violation still go on, the whole body would suffer in a degree, but the finger most of all. I remove the cord, and the swollen flesh subsides. It is purple no longer. The pain and uneasiness are gone. There is a lesson for you in this, Mr. Holbrook. Does the text of my illustration need a paraphrase?"

"Go on," said the merchant.

"You are the congested finger."

"What?"

"You have received, and are receiving, of this world's goods, more than you can possibly use in any orderly way of life; looking, simply, to the common needs and demands of yourself and family. Is it not so? Think."

"I am rich," said Mr. Holbrook; "but my riches have come through honorable devotion to business. Trade, not trick and speculation, has filled my coffers. There is no stain on my escutcheon."

"I can believe that, Sir, and yet I see you as a congested, and not a healthy working member of the common social body. So far as you are engaged in useful merchandising, so far you are acting in an orderly relation. But, are not you regarding yourself alone, in your employments and accumulations? Do you ever soberly think of use to others, or seek to serve others. Like your eye and hand, do you see for the whole and work for the whole?"

"If I get your drift," said the merchant, "you would have me scatter my wealth in charitable deeds, and thus get rid of the congestion to which you refer."

"No."

"What then?"

"I would have you," replied the friend, "first turn your eyes away from yourself, and out upon the great social body of which you form a part. It is a diseased body, because its members are more or less diseased. Its great heart beats in quick, strong, feverish pulsations, sending the poorly vitalized blood through obstructed channels. Endowed with large means and influence, you have power to do good in a wider range than most men. You can aid this common body in its efforts towards a higher and truer life; and in thus giving unselfish aid, states of tranquillity and deep interior peace will come to you as a reward."

Mr. Holbrook cast his eyes upon the ground and sat for some time in thoughtful silence.

"I see a glimmer of truth in what you say," he remarked, looking up at his friend. "Society is held together, and sustained by a great system of reciprocal uses; though men, in entering into them, are moved only by selfish instincts."

"But," said the friend, "if a generous regard for the neighbor governed all men in their employments, they would work from a higher principle and have a higher reward. While no less prosperous, an inward delight would flow from possession as the correspondent of good service done to others."

"A dream of Arcadia." Mr. Holbrook smiled. His friend answered:

"No, simply an image of society in right order; that is, as God designed it to be; and as it must be, ere true happiness can dwell among the sons of man. My dear old friend," added the visitor, "let me give you this great truth on which to ponder; you will see it clearer, I trust, hereafter, than now. *Just in the degree that men regard the good of others in their feelings, thoughts, and actions, will they be happy; and in just the degree that they regard only themselves, will they be miserable.* We must, like healthy bodily organs, do our part for the common good, or we will become morally congested and diseased; and of course, bear about with us perpetual states of disquietude or pain. The truth which I have given you to ponder, is based on the laws of social life and order originally ordained of God. As we depart from these, must not a consequence be pain? In the degree that we keep them, must not happiness fill our hearts? The proposition needs no forcing—no illustration—it is simply self-evident."

"I will think on what you have said," answered the merchant. "It sounded strangely at first; but I see it differently now. Alas! how far from the true paths our feet have wandered, and the way back has no attractions."

"No attractions," was replied, "while we think only of ourselves; but, if we permit our hearts to go out in a generous regard for others, we shall soon find it a pleasant, flower strewn way. Then, and then only, will we begin to comprehend the true meaning of a word that is on all lips; and of a state after which every human heart aspires with irrepressible longings."

V.

DARKEST BEFORE DAY.

THROUGH many sore life-trials he had passed. Death had come in once, twice, thrice; and as often, a little mound, measuring only a few feet in length, had arisen, greenly, in the graveyard.

These were sorrows that Edward Walker accepted as from the hand of God; and he bowed his head submissively, through tears. It was hard, very hard to part with his heart and household treasures; but, the language of consolation was distinctly uttered, and his ears hearkened to the preacher's voice—hearkened, while his soul responded—"The Lord gave, and the Lord taketh away; blessed be the name of the Lord."

For such wounds, the heart finds balm in Gilead. There are sources of consolation on every hand. Though we miss the sweet young faces, and our hearts yearn for the voices that shall sound in our dwellings no more, we have an assurance which nothing can obliterate, that our precious ones are in Heaven. We would not recall them. Though the pang of parting was severe, it endured only for a brief season. On the darkness of affliction, morning broke, and the sun of Righteousness arose with healing in his wings.

Edward Walker had drained this cup of sorrow even to the bitter dregs; and yet walked forth, submissive, patient, leaning, as he believed, on God.

"Though He slay me, yet will I trust in Him." So he felt—so he spoke; strong in conscious spiritual strength.

"God is my refuge; a present help in time of trouble." How often had he said this, looking upward, and believing in his own unfaltering trust.

"Though I walk through the valley of the shadow of death, I will fear no evil." Even onwards to the dark hour of mortal extremity he had looked, and believed himself strong enough in the strength of a Christian to meet the last trial.

Yet, for all this, Edward Walker's trust in God was more a pious fervor than a living principle. It was not based on a true understanding of the laws of spiritual life. He was worldly-minded to a degree far beyond any thing imagined in his own heart. His serene life flowed as much from a consciousness of fair standing with society and his brethren in the church, as from any quality of goodness that he possessed—nay, more. He was a prominent man in his sect; and dutiful in every work that came to his hand; but the leaven of self-righteousness was in all his deeds, though he knew it not. He had, really, more of the man-pleasing, than the God-fearing element in his formally religious life.

Mr. Walker had borne, with patient resignation, the death of children, the loss of worldly goods, the estrangement of friends; but a deeper trial awaited him—he must go down into the valley of humiliation. The fair name he had borne so proudly in the eyes of his brethren, and the world, must be sullied. His motives, honest and honorable, must be impugned:—He must take, for a time, a false position, and bear unjust judgment, contumely and wrong. Ah! This was a fiery trial indeed. Who can meet it without a shrinking fear?

A false friend won the confidence of Mr. Walker, and prevailed on him to become surety for a large amount; and thus he became involved in obligations far beyond his means. Under promises from this friend to reimburse him at an early day, he borrowed from members of the church to which he belonged, various sums, with which he lifted the obligations at maturity. Then he discovered that he was in the hands of an unscrupulous villain; and that he was in danger of not only losing every thing he possessed, but of falling largely in debt to his brethren in the church.

All trust in God died out in the heart of Mr. Walker. He saw night, impenetrable night closing round him. His good name, which had been so dear, was tarnished. Church members passed him in the street with averted faces, or nodded coldly. All the old firm places on which he had stood so confidently, were mire beneath his feet. And yet, he struggled desperately amid the wrecks of hope and fortune; struggled with the wild, but uncertain strength of the despairing.

But all availed not. His ship went under, bearing to ocean depths every thing he had held most precious in this life.

"I cannot bear this," he said to his wife, a woman whose spiritual perceptions were clearer than his, because her thought was less in the world and more in duty. Yet, for lack of a more pious exterior, she had many times suffered rebuke, even from his lips. "I cannot bear it, Hannah. The trial is too great."

All he possessed had gone into the Sheriff's hands, and on that day was to be sacrificed and scattered.

"Look up, and trust in God, Edward,"

"I cannot bear it, Hannah!"

was her trembling reply. "He is still in Heaven. He will not forsake you in the hour of trial and darkness."

"He has already forsaken me!" was bitterly answered.

"I have been young, and now am I old; yet have I not seen the righteous forsaken, nor his seed begging bread." Mrs. Walker repeated this comforting assurance of Holy Writ; but her husband rejected it bitterly.

"I have leaned upon an uncertain reed, and in breaking, it has pierced," he said.

"But that reed was not God's truth," replied his wife, calmly. "God's truth is a rock, and cannot break. Dear husband, look upwards! Let not your faith fail now. The night has fallen upon us. It is dark—very dark—but, day must be at hand. After the night, then cometh morning."

"Don't talk to me, Hannah! Your words come to my ears like mocking sounds. Have I not been faithful in all my religious duties? Have I not been a praying man, and a worker in God's vineyard? Who was more instant in season and out of season than I? Whose life has been more blameless? And yet, such hypocrites as you and I know Lloyd, and Black, and Somers to be, draw away from me in righteous reproof, or pass to the other side, lest I contaminate them by a touch!"

"God looks at the heart," said Mrs. Walker, calmly, and with a Christian assurance that showed how her life was grounded. "And if we are right with God we need not fear what men can do unto us. Did you purpose in your heart to wrong any one?"

"No—God is my witness, no!" Mr. Walker, in conscious innocence and weakness, made then, spontaneously, his appeal to Heaven.

"Is it not better to stand well with God than with men? to have the heart's honor unstained? O, my husband, look up! Trust all in the hands of Him who loves us with no blind human regard, but with an infinitely wise and tender love. His ways are not as our ways—He sees not as we see. If He calls us to walk through the fire, it is because we need purification."

Mr. Walker had been the monitor heretofore. Standing erect, in conscious religious strength, he had been the enunciator of life precepts, the reprover, the encourager; while his wife had leaned towards him, and received, meekly, into her heart the lessons he gave. But now he was weak and despairing as a stricken child, while she stood up, strong in her unwavering reliance upon God. Mr. Walker felt the contrast, and it rebuked him. He saw, in her life, an element of spiritual power to which he was a stranger. Half in surprise at an attempt on her part to give him strength in so great an extremity, he had answered: "Don't talk to me, Hannah!" But her perception and confidence appeared, now, in such contrast with his blindness and loss of trust, that his weak heart turned to her with hope's shattered wings lifting themselves, as for an upward flight again.

"The God of Daniel never sleeps," said

Mrs. Walker. "He is the same God—yesterday, to-day, and forever. The lions can have no power over them that serve him with pure hearts, fervently. This is our time of darkness, Edward—our last day of strong trial. To-morrow it will be light again. A new day will dawn; and though our feet may not find the way so flowery as it has been, nor over such a level ground, yet will it be broad, bright day, my husband. We shall see the sun again—the sun of righteousness—rising for us, with healing on his wings. Go out, then, to-day, Edward—to-day, though the sky is all overclouded, and the rain falls coldly and drearily. Meet its trials and its duties, trusting in God, and fearing no mortal. Let a sense of rectitude sustain you in the face of your enemies. Stand up, bravely, as a Christian man. See that no one suffers through an abandonment of your post, in this critical juncture of affairs. Some of the very men who affect pious scorn of you, because, in your helpless embarrassment, you can no more keep your pledged word than a chained man can run a race—some of these men, I say, will not scruple to take advantage of your indifference to gather more than their share of the property to be scattered to-day. Stand firm in the breach, then; stand firm, and receive the last shock, as a true Christian soldier. Let God and the right be your motto; and just so surely as the darkness has closed, will the day dawn upon us."

Thus enjoined, Mr. Walker, who had, in his weak, man-fearing spirit, determined to shut himself away from all eyes on this day of humiliation and disaster, went forth in a new strength, born of the true words spoken by his wife. It was after nightfall when he came home. Anxiously did his suffering but patient companion look into his face when he opened the door and came in, almost noiseless. How the old firm step had failed! That face was pale, exhausted, sad.

"Dear Edward! How is it with you?" said Mrs. Walker, laying her hands upon him, and gazing into his eyes, with her own full of tender sympathy and undying love.

"Better than I had feared, Hannah."

Light flushed over her face.

"Oh, Edward!" She laid her head down upon his bosom for a moment or two. When she looked up rainbows were in her eyes.

"Yes, dear," he answered, the sad look fading from around his lips. "It has not proved such hopeless ruin as I had feared, thanks to your inspiriting words this morning. If I had remained in weakness and abandonment of duty at home, the disaster would have been complete. Two hours before the sale was to take place, I discovered that an understanding existed between three or four of my creditors not to bid against each other, but to suffer every thing to be knocked off at the meagerest prices. Through their management, and the connivance of the deputy-sheriff, a wrong hour for the sale had been inserted in bills and advertisements, so that no company of rival bidders could be in attendance. Becoming aware of this, I called personally upon every other creditor, and upon a large number of business men, strangers as well as acquaintances, who could have any possible interest in the sale, and advised all of the dishonest course which had been adopted; naming, in all cases, the men engaged therein, so that they might be known. In consequence of this prompt action on my part, a very large company, in sympathy with me as a man against whom wrong was intended, were on the ground, and every item of property brought very close to its market value—so close, Hannah, that I shall not be in debt. Every man will get his own."

"It was dark, Edward—very dark," said Mrs. Walker in tears—"but I knew the day would break."

"It is breaking, dear," he replied, in a subdued manner; "but not yet in the natural east. I do not see the morning dawn of worldly hope. I am sitting in darkness. The way before me is all obstruction. I am down in a deep valley, and a mountain that seems impassable obstructs my way. But over the hill-tops of my spiritual east light is coming. I see the hand of a Divine benevolence in this sore trial of the natural man. I trusted in myself, when I fancied my trust was in the Lord; I was serene of spirit, because I stood well with men; the praise of my brethren was dearer to me than the approval of God. I was self-righteous, Hannah—meanly and poorly self-righteous. And when the hand of misfortune was laid upon me, when my good name and my honor among men were touched, I had no strength to stand. I was not strong in the consciousness of a righteous purpose. But, thanks to God for the trial, which has showed me a true image of myself. I will be patient, hopeful, humble I trust, while it may please Him that I walk in this harder way of life. Over the sunny mountains of celestial love the morning star has arisen. I see its pure radiance, falling on my path, and showing me a better way. Night has departed. Dark, tearful, despairing night. I have passed through a fearful trial; but the storm is behind me, and mutters now in the far away distance."

Mrs. Walker saw a light in her husband's face such as she had never seen before; a light which came after the darkness of human despair into which the weak heart, that trusted only in self and the world, falls when the days of trouble come. She smiled serenely and hopefully upon him, as she answered in words of Divine encouragement, that, familiar as they had been from childhood, fell upon his ears like a new revelation of God's love:

"The Lord is my shepherd; I shall not want. He maketh me to lie down in green pastures; he leadeth me in the paths of righteousness for his name's sake. Yea, though I walk through the valley of the shadow of death, I will fear no evil; for thou art with me; thy rod and thy staff they comfort me. Thou preparest a table before me in the presence of mine enemies; thou anointest my head with oil; my cup runneth over. Surely goodness and mercy shall follow me all the days of my life: and I shall dwell in the house of the Lord forever."

VI.

MY WHISTLING NEIGHBOR.

We had moved into a new house, situated about the center in a row of ten, all run up together in hurried, mushroom fashion, and divided from each other by partitions of brick so thin that sound was only a little deadened in passing through. For the first three or four nights I was unable to sleep, except in snatches, for so many noises came to my ears, originating, apparently, in my own domicile, that anxiety in regard to burglars was constantly excited. Both on the first and second nights I made a journey through the house in the small hours, but found no intruders on my premises. The sounds that disturbed me came from some of my neighbors, who kept later vigils than suited my habits.

"There it is again!" said I, looking up from my paper, as I sat reading on the second day after taking possession of my new home. "That fellow is a nuisance."

"What fellow?" asked my wife, whose countenance showed surprise at the remark. She was either unconscious or unaffected by the circumstance that annoyed my sensitive ears.

"Don't you hear it?" said I.

"Hear what?"

"That everlasting whistle."

"Oh!" A smile played over my wife's face. "Does it annoy you?"

"I can't say that I am particularly annoyed by it yet; but I shall be if it's to go on incessantly. A man whistles for want of thought, and this very fact will—"

"I'm not so sure of that," remarked my wife, interrupting me, "the poet notwithstanding. I would say that he whistles from exuberant feelings. Our neighbor has a sunny temper, no doubt; what, I am afraid, cannot be said of our neighbor on the other side. I've never heard him whistle; but his scolding abilities are good, and, judging from two days' observation, he is not likely to permit them to grow feeble for want of use."

I did not answer, but went on with my reading, silenced if not reconciled to my whistling neighbor.

Business matters annoyed me through the day, and I felt moody and depressed as I took my course homeward at nightfall. I was not leaving my cares behind me. Before shutting my account-books, and locking my fire-proof, I had made up a bundle of troubles to carry away with me, and my shoulders stooped beneath the burden.

I did not bring sunlight into my dwelling as I crossed, with dull, deliberate steps, its threshold. The flying feet that sprung along the hall, and the eager voices that filled, suddenly, the air in a sweet tumult of sound as I entered, were quiet and hushed in a little while. I did not repel my precious ones, for they were very dear to my heart; but birds do not sing joyously except in the sunshine, and my presence had cast a shadow. The songs of my home birds had died into fitful chirpings—they sat quiet among the branches. I saw this, and understood the reason. I condemned myself; I reasoned against the folly of bringing worldly cares into the home sanctuary; I endeavored to rise out of my gloomy state. But neither philosophy nor a self-compelling effort was of any avail.

I was sitting, with my hand partly shading my face from the light, still in conflict with myself, when I became conscious of a lifting of the shadows that were around me, and of a freer respiration. The change was slight, but still very perceptible. I was beginning to question as to its cause, when my thought recognized an agency which had been operative through the sense of hearing, though not before externally perceived in consequence of my abstracted state. My neighbor was whistling "Begone, Dull Care!"

Now, in my younger days, I had whistled and sung the air and words of this cheerful old song hundreds of times, and every line was familiar to memory. I listened with pleased interest, for a little while, and then, as my changing state gave power to resolutions quick born of better reason, I said, in my thought, emphatically, as if remanding an evil spirit,

"Begone, dull care!" And the fiend left me.

Then I spoke cheerfully, and in a tone of interest to quiet little May, who had walked round me three or four times, wondering in her little heart, no doubt, what held her at a distance from her papa, and who was now seated by her mother, leaning her flaxen head, fluted all over with glossy curls, against her knee. She sprung at my voice, and was in my lap at a bound. What a thrill of pleasure the tight clasp of her arms sent to my heart! Oh love, thou art full of blessing!

From that moment I felt kinder toward my neighbor. He had done me good—had played before me as David pláyed before Saul, exorcising the evil spirit of discontent. There was no longer a repellent sphere, and soon all my little ones were close around me, and happy as in other times with their father.

After they were all in bed, and I sat alone with my wife, the cares that "infest the day" made a new assault upon me, and vigorously strove to regain their lost empire in my mind. I felt their approaches, and the gradual receding of cheerful thoughts with every advancing step they made. In my struggle to maintain that tranquillity which so strengthens the soul for work and duty, I arose and walked the floor. My wife looked up to me with inquiry on her face. Then she let her eyes fall upon her needle-work, and as I glanced toward her at every turn in my walk, I saw an expression of tender concern on her lips. She understood that I was not at ease in my mind, and the knowledge troubled her.

"How wrong in me," I said, in self-rebuke, "thus to let idle brooding over mere outside things, which such brooding can in no way effect, trouble the peace of home;" and I made a new effort to rise again into a sunnier region. But the fiend had me in his clutches again, and I could not release myself. Now it was that my David came anew to my relief.

Suddenly his clear notes rang out in the air, "Away with Melancholy."

I cannot tell which worked the instant revulsion of feeling that came—the cheerful air, the words of the song which were called to remembrance by the air, or the associations of by-gone years that were revived. But the spell was potent and complete. I was myself again.

During the evening the voice of my wife broke out several times into snatches of song —a thing quite unusual of late, for life's sober realities had taken the music from her as well as from her husband. We were growing graver every day. It was pleasant to hear her flute-tones again, very pleasant, and my ear hearkened lovingly. The cause of this fitful warbling I recognized each time as the notes died away. They were responsive to our neighbor.

I did not then remark upon the circumstance. One reason of this lay in the fact that I had spoken lightly of our neighbor's whistling propensity, which struck me in the beginning as vulgar; and I did not care to acknowledge myself so largely his debtor as I really was.

We were in our bedroom, and about retiring for the night, when loud voices, as if in strife, came discordantly through the thin party walls, from our neighbors on the other side. Something had gone wrong there, and angry passions were in the ascendant.

"How very disagreeable!" I remarked.

"The man's a brute!" said my wife emphatically. "He does nothing, it seems to me, but wrangle in his family. Pity he hadn't something of the pleasant temper of our neighbor on the other side."

"That is a more agreeable sound, I must confess," was my answer as the notes of "What Fairy like Music steals over the Sea" rose sweetly on the air.

"Far more agreeable," returned my wife.

"He plays well on his instrument," I said, smiling. My ear was following the notes in pleased recognition. We stood listening until our neighbor passed to another air, set to Mrs. Hemans's beautiful words, "Come to the Sunset Tree." To a slow, soft, tender measure the notes fell, yet still we heard them with singular distinctness through the intervening wall, just a little muffled, but sweeter for the obstruction.

> "The Day is past and gone,
> The woodman's axe lies free,
> And the reaper's work is done."

My wife recalled these lines from her memory, repeating them in a subdued, tranquilizing tone. The air was still sounding in our ears, but we no longer recognized its impression on the external senses. It had done its work of recalling the beautiful Evening Hymn of the Switzer, and we repeated to each other verse after verse.

> "Sweet is the hour of rest,
> Pleasant the wood's low sigh,
> And the gleaming of the west,
> And the turf whereon we lie.
> When the burden and the heat
> Of labor's task are o'er,
> And kindly voices greet
> The loved one at the door."

To which I added:

"But rest, more sweet and still
  Than ever nightfall gave,
Our longing hearts shall fill
  In the world beyond the grave.
There shall no tempest blow,
  No scorching noontide beat;
There shall be no more snow,
  No weary, wandering feet;
And we lift our trusting eyes
  From the hills our fathers trod,
To the quiet of the skies—
  To the Sabbath of our God."

All was now still on both sides. The harsh discord of our scolding neighbor had ceased, and our whistling neighbor had warbled his good-night melody, which, like a pleasant flower growing near an unsightly object, and interposing a veil of beauty, had removed it from our consciousness.

It was a long time since I had felt so peaceful on retiring as when my head went down upon its pillow—thanks to my light-hearted neighbor, at whose whistling propensities I was inclined in the beginning to be annoyed. But for him I should have gone to rest with the harsh discord of my scolding neighbor's voice in my ears, and been ill at ease with myself and the world. On what seeming trifles hang our states of mind! A word, a look, a tone of music, a discordant jar, will bring light or shadow, smiles or tears.

On the next morning, while dressing myself, thought reached forward over the day's anxieties, and care began drawing her sombre curtains around me. My neighbor was stirring also, and, like the awaking bird, tuneful in sweet matins. "Day on the Mountains" rang out cheerily, followed by "Dear Summer Morn;" winding off with "Begone, Dull Care!" and the merry laughter of a happy child which had sprung into his arms, and was being smothered with kisses.

The cloud that was gathering on my brow passed away, and I met my wife and children at the breakfast-table with pleasant smiles.

In a few days I ceased to notice the whistling of my neighbor. It continued as usual; but had grown to be such a thing of course as not to be an object of thought. But the effect remained, showing itself in a gradual restoration of that cheerfulness which care, and work, and brooding anxiety about worldly things are so apt to produce. The "voice of music," which had been almost dumb in my wife for a long period, was gradually restored. Old familiar ditties would break suddenly from her throat as she sat sewing, and I would often hear her singing again, from room to room, as in the sunnier days of our spring-time. As for myself, scarcely an evening passed in which I was not betrayed into beating time with my foot to "Auld Lang Syne," "Happy Land," "Comin' through the Rye," or "Hail Columbia," in response to my neighbor's cheery whistle. Our children also caught the infection, and would commence singing on the instant our neighbor tuned his pipes. Verily he was our benefactor—the harping David to our Saul!

"You live at number 510, I think," said a gentleman whose face was familiar, though I was not able to call his name. We were sitting side by side in the cars.

I answered in the affirmative.

"So I thought," he replied. "I live at 514—second door east."

"Mr. Gordon."

"Yes, Sir; that is my name. Pleasant houses, but mere shells," said he. Then, with a look of disgust on his face, "Doesn't that whistling fellow between us annoy you terribly? I've got so out of all patience that I shall either move or silence him. Whistle, whistle, whistle, from morning till night. Pah! I always detested whistling. It's a sign of no brains. I've written him a note twice, but failed to send either time; it isn't well to quarrel with a neighbor if you can help it."

"It doesn't annoy me at all," I answered. "Indeed, I rather like it."

"You do? Well, that is singular! Just what my wife says."

"First-rate for the blue devils, I find. I'm indebted to our whistling friend for sundry favors in this direction."

My new acquaintance looked at me curiously.

"You're not in earnest," said he, a half-amused smile breaking through the unamiable expression which his face had assumed.

"Altogether in earnest; and I beg of you not to send him that note. So your wife is not annoyed?"

"Not she."

"Is she musical?" I inquired.

"She was; but of late years life has been rather a serious matter with us, and her singing birds have died, or lost the heart for music."

"The history of many other lives," said I.

The man sighed faintly.

"Has there been any recent change?" I ventured to inquire.

"In what respect?" he asked.

"Has there been no voice from the singing birds?"

A new expression came suddenly into the man's face.

"Why, yes," he answered, "now that I think of it. There has been some low, fitful warblings. Only last evening the voice of my wife stole out, as if half afraid, and trembled a little while on the words of an old song."

"The air of which our neighbor was whistling at the time," said I.

"Right, as I live!" was my companion's exclamation, after a pause, slapping his hand on his knee. I could hardly help smiling at the look of wonder, amusement, and conviction that blended on his face.

"I wouldn't send that note," said I meaningly.

"No, hang me if I do! I must study this case. I'm something of a philosopher, you must know. If our neighbor can awaken the singing birds in the heart of my wife, he may whistle till the crack of doom without hindrance from me. I'm obliged to you for the suggestion."

A week afterward I met him again.

"What about the singing birds?" I asked, smiling.

"All alive again, thank God!" He answered with a heartiness of manner that caused me to look narrowly into his face. It wore a better expression than when I observed it last.

"Then you didn't send that note?"

"No, Sir. Why, since I saw you I've actually taken to whistling and humming old tunes again, and you can't tell how much better it makes me feel. And the children are becoming as merry and musical as crickets. Our friend's whistle sets them all agoing, like the first signal-warble of a bird at day-dawn that awakens the woods to melody."

We were on our way homeward, and parted at my own door. As I entered "Home, Sweet Home" was pulsing in tender harmonies on the air. I stood still and listened until tears fell over my cheeks. The singing birds were alive again in the heart of my wife also, and I said "Thank God!" as warmly as my neighbor had uttered the words a little while before.

VII.

HONEY *vs.* VINEGAR.

"He shall do it, Mr. Jackson! I'll let him see who is strongest. I'll take the conceit out of him. No man shall ride over me after this fashion."

The speaker, a farmer named Milwood, was in a state of considerable excitement, as may be inferred from his language. There was trouble between him and a neighboring farmer named Bland, about a pair of steers which Milwood had bought from the latter, but which, on a trial, proved unsound. He had sent them back by one of his men, who delivered an irritating message, in a very irritating way. In consequence, the steers were returned to Mr. Milwood, with a stinging response; covering an intimation, that if he did not wish to get himself into trouble, he'd better keep the animals.

Post haste, Mr. Milwood started for the office of Mr. Jackson, a lawyer of the better class, who never encouraged fruitless litigation among his neighbors for the sake of fees; stated his case under a strong head of excitement, and desired the immediate initiation of compulsory measures.

"Take a little time for thought, Mr. Milwood," said the lawyer, after getting a confused and voluble statement of the case. "Bland is as stubborn as a mule if you attempt to drive him."

"I don't care if he's as stubborn as forty mules; he shall take back that pair of steers. Jack Milwood is not the man to be juggled after this fashion."

"He'll never do it, if you attempt to drive him, Mr. Milwood. I've had one or two bouts with him; and he is the hardest kind of a customer. Go to law and it will cost you both the price of half a dozen steers, twice told, before you are through.'

"He shall do it, Mr. Jackson," answered Mr. Milwood, in the sentence with which our story opens. "I'll let him see who is strongest. I'll take the conceit out of him. No man shall ride over me after this fashion."

"There are always two sides to a question," said the lawyer, "and one sounds very well until the other is stated. Judges and juries understand this as well as most people. Plaintiff and defendant, each looking only at his own side of a case, are generally confident of winning; bnt no result is to be calculated on with certainty. We can't always make judges and juries see with our eyes. Take my advice, and arrange this matter with Bland. Don't let it find its way into court. I think he's a reasonable man, when not blind and stubborn through excited feeling."

"He's a cheat!" ejaculated Milwood, with indignant warmth. "He knew the steers were unsound when he sold them. Fortunately, I've not paid for them yet; and I'll spend every dollar I'm worth before he shall collect their price from me."

"If that is the case," said the lawyer, "let me counsel a 'masterly inactivity' on your part, rather than offensive demonstrations. Wait until he attempts to force a collection. But, I trust, sober second thought will lead you to seek a compromise of the matter with Mr. Bland."

"A compromise! Never, sir." And Mr. Milwood retired from Mr. Jackson's office in no better state of mind than when he entered. On his way home, he met Mr. Bland.

"Look here, sir!" he said angrily, "that was a clean swindle. You knew—"

But Mr. Bland turned from his assailant, and without a word of reply, walked away. His face was pale from suppressed feeling; his hands clenched so tightly that the nails almost cut into the flesh; his teeth set into a kind of vehement determination to punish the outrage which he had just suffered. To be charged with swindling his neighbor! This was beyond forgiveness!

"He'll be sorry for that, till the day of doom," he muttered, almost savagely, as he strode homeward. "A swindle, indeed! And I a swindler, of course—a rogue—a cheat! That's talking on the square. By all that's good and bad, he shall eat his words if it cost me every dollar I'm worth!"

On his way home, farmer Bland met his neighbor, named Jenkins, to whom, under considerable excitement, he told the story of his trouble with Milwood.

"Oh he's a cranky sort of a man, and always was; one of the kind that rides rough shod over the people, if they're fool enough to let him. He tried his game of bluster with me once upon a time, but you may take my word for it, he came off second best."

"As he will again," retorted the farmer. "There never was a sounder pair of steers than those he bought from me; he's got to keep them. If he'd behaved like a decent man about it, he might have had his way. If he'd come to me as one neighbor ought always to come to another, and said, 'Mr. Bland, I'm afraid the steers wont suit me,' or 'I don't think they're sound,' and asked me in the right way to receive them back again, there'd never been a word between us. But, to send them home, with an impudent message, wasn't the way to deal with Silas Bland."

Now this Jenkins, to whom Mr. Bland was venting his indignation, was not a prudent neighbor, but a meddler in strifes. He took an evil kind of pleasure in fanning the flames of discord, instead of seeking to extinguish them. After parting with Mr. Bland he fell in with Milwood.

"Hallo, old fellow!" was his rude salutation. "What's up with you and Bland?"

"Who said any thing was up with us?" replied Milwood, who was already beginning to feel, since his meeting with Bland, a little regret for the rough way in which he had assailed him. Though hasty and passionate, and given to unreasonable bluster in the outset of an unpleasant matter, in cooler moments he was a right thinking and a right feeling man.

"I met Bland himself, just now," replied Jenkins, "and he's as mad as a March hare. I rather think he means to put you through."

"If he isn't put through himself," said Milwood, his mind growing turbulent again.

"What's the trouble?" asked Jenkins.

"Oh, he tried to put off on me, a pair of miserable steers that I wouldn't give stable room. A downright swindle!"

"He'll take them back, if not sound, of course."

"Not he!"

"I'd make him," said Jenkins.

"That's just what I'm going to do."

"I always thought him tricky and unscrupulous," added Jenkins, by way of helping his neighbor to as antagonistic a state of mind as possible; "and I hope he'll get a lesson this time that he'll remember for half a dozen years at least."

"He will, you may depend on it, if he doesn't get out of my way. I'm kind of riled up from the bottom at the mean attempt to cheat me; and when I'm riled up, I'm a sort of ugly customer, as Silas Bland will find to his cost.

So the breach was widened by one indiscreet and meddlesome neighbor after another, until farmer Bland was induced to enter suit against Milwood for recovery of the price of the steers. They, in the mean time, were standing idle, in Mr. Milwood's stable, enjoying good feed and leisure; the price of their board being regularly charged, every week, by Mr. Milwood, against Mr. Bland, and it was his intention to sue him for the bill, after the case was decided against his neighbor, as he doubted not it would be.

Bland had called first on lawyer Jackson; but that right-minded gentleman having discouraged litigation in the case, another, and less scrupulous limb of the law was found; and by him proceedings were begun. He saw a charming entanglement ahead; and one likely to afford a year or two of pleasant and profitable service for himself. Mr. Bland was a farmer in easy circumstances, and could afford to pay costs and fees. So he made him believe he was a shamefully injured man; and read him decisions from the law books which showed his case to be of the clearest kind and certain to end favorably.

"I am sorry about this matter, neighbor Milwood," said lawyer Jackson, when he was called upon to defend the suit. "I think it might have been arranged without going to law, and making more bad blood between you."

"But what can I do, Mr. Jackson? The animals are not sound."

"Have you seen Mr. Bland?"

"No, sir, of course not! After all that has passed, I can't go to see him.

"It would be best, I think, Mr. Milwood."

"Why should I see him?"

"In order to settle the matter between yourselves, like sensible men and good neighbors."

"Why didn't he call on me before commencing this suit? I'm the party aggrieved. He knows why I refused to pay for the steers. It isn't my place to go to him."

"I think differently, Mr. Milwood."

"And I am surprised to hear you say so, Mr. Jackson."

"The first provocation was on your side."

"On my side! I'm astonished to hear you say that."

Mr. Milwood really looked surprised.

"When you discovered that the animals were unsound, what did you do?"

"I sent them back."

"Before seeing Mr. Bland on the subject?"

"Yes."

"And with the animals you sent a message?"

"Yes."

"What was it?"

"I don't just remember now."

"Not a very pleasant one, I presume?"

"Perhaps not. I wasn't in the most agreeable humor in the world. The attempt to foist upon me a pair of indifferent steers annoyed me."

"You sent word that you wouldn't take them for their hide and tallow."

"No, sir."

"That and other irritating things were said by your man."

"If so, they were said on his own responsibility."

"But, remember, they were received as coming from you, through your messenger. Now, I don't wonder that Mr. Bland was annoyed. You would have been made angry and resistant under similar circumstances. These sharp sayings between neighbors are not good, and lead to a great deal of unnecessary trouble, as in the present case. Had you, on finding the steers not satisfactory, gone to Mr. Bland, and in a right spirit, stated the case, there would have been no trouble. He would have said: 'Very well, neighbor Milwood: if you are not entirely satisfied, send them home."

"No, sir; I don't believe a word of it! He got a bad bargain off his hands, and meant to stick to it through thick and thin. I've heard all about them steers. He only bought them a week before they were sold to me; and finding them good for nothing, deliberately swindled me."

"Now, don't permit yourself to use such

hard language against your neighbor," said the lawyer. "I don't believe Mr. Bland had any intention to swindle you. All this trouble is of your own brewing. There is too much acid about you, Mr. Milwood; pardon me for saying so. Too much vinegar and too little honey. Now, it's a proverb as old as the hills, that honey catches more flies than vinegar; and you'll find it true in the present case. You've tried vinegar on Mr. Bland, and it hasn't worked well; try the honey, and my word for it you'll find it acting like a charm."

"You don't mean that I shall go and humble myself to Mr. Bland!"

"Nonsense! Humbling! No man humbles himself in doing right. If you have made a mistake, correct it; that is manly. You are very angry at Mr. Bland for not correcting his mistake in selling you a pair of steers not up to the representation. Set him the good example of correcting your own error, and my word for it, he will follow suit, instantly, and your stormy sky will be clear again. Go to him now, in a kind, neighborly, Christian spirit, as you should have done in the beginning. Let him see the gentle and reasonable side of your character. Talk with him as a man to his brother. Use honey instead of gall, or vinegar, and then, if he will not do what is right and just, come to me, and I will undertake to defend your case."

Mr. Milwood retired from the lawyer's office in a better state of mind than any that had ruled him since the beginning of the trouble. He saw, as he had never seen before, his own wrong position. Mentally, he placed himself on the other side: and then it was clear to him, that if Mr. Bland had sent him back the steers with a rough and insulting message, such as his man had delivered, he would have revolted at it in a similar way. Most men can be led, and few driven.

But, it was a hard thing for Mr. Milwood to make up his mind to call on farmer Bland. There was something in this galling to his pride—something that, in spite of his better reason, he felt to be humiliating. Mr. Bland would think he was frightened by a suit, and feel that he had humbled him. On leaving Mr. Jackson's office, Mr. Milwood had done so with more than a half formed purpose to call on his neighbor ; but suggestions of this kind threw him into another state of mind. He felt that he could not do it. That any consequence which might come would be preferable to that humiliation. He was walking along with his eyes bent on the ground, still in mental doubt, and with better arguments gaining influence in his mind, when he heard the sound of feet, and glancing up, saw Mr. Bland only a few rods ahead of him. It was the first time they had looked fairly into each other's faces since the beginning of this trouble. Mr. Milwood's feet were checked instantly. He stood still, and looked calmly –what an effort it cost him !—at his neighbor, whose countenance was hard, defiant, angry. Mr. Bland paused also.

"There is one thing I wish to say to you, and am glad of this opportunity," said Mr. Milwood. His tone was serious.

"Say on, sir!" The farmer was as cold and repellant as an iceberg.

"There is only one right way to atone for errors, and that is to undo them if you can."

"Well, sir!" The farmer did not relax in the smallest degree.

"In the beginning of the unfortunate trouble, I was wrong in one thing."

"Ah!" A sudden change in the hard exterior of Mr. Bland was visible.

"I should have called to talk the matter over with you, in a neighborly way, before sending home the steers. I acted from a first impulse; and have been sorry for it since."

"If you had done that, Mr. Milwood," replied the other, in a frank, earnest way, "there would have been no trouble between us. I believe myself to be an honest man at heart; and am always ready to do right when I am shown to be in error."

By an involuntary movement, the two men's right hands commenced approaching each other, and were clasped before either had recalled the thought of a present reconciliation—clasped and held tightly, in a mutual pressure. As they stood, thus, looking at each other, the hardness and anger went out of their faces; and the old softness and neighborly interest came back.

"Anger is a bad counsellor," said Mr. Milwood, in a kind, yet serious voice.

"A very bad counsellor, friend Milwood," replied the neighbor; "and if you are agreed, we will dismiss him now, and take Good Will in his place. Under his better guidance, I am sure we can settle this matter to our mutual satisfaction. The failure to do so shall be no fault of mine."

"Nor mine," answered Mr. Milwood.

"I sold you those steers," said the farmer, "in good faith. I was not aware of any thing being wrong with them. But if it is as you allege, send them home, and let the affair end here. I am glad to have met you."

"Ah, neighbor Bland; I see, now, in what a foolish way I acted," replied Mr. Milwood. "This taking it for granted that another means to do wrong, is neither just nor generous. We'll look at the steers together. Perhaps it isn't as bad as I've imagined."

"You shall have it just as you will," said Mr. Bland—"only let us be friends as of old."

And the matter was settled between them in less than an hour, to mutual satisfaction. Both were right at heart. Both honest, and willing to concede under mild influences; but quick-tempered, proud and stubborn under provocation. There are thousands like them, who are enemies to-day, yet should be friends—enemies, because anger, instead of neighborly good will, has been taken into the heart as a counsellor. If any such are readers of this story, let them act at once from the better impulses we may hope it has quickened in their hearts.

VIII.

POOR COUSIN EUNICE.

"I HAVE a letter from Windham," said Mr. Gregory. It was nearly five minutes after he had come in, one cold Saturday evening in November. A fire had been made up in the dining-room, and his wife and two oldest daughters, Harriet and Lizzy, were sitting in its genial glow when he entered, and joined the circle that opened to receive him.

"From Helen?"

"No. Helen is dead."

"Dead?"

There was surprise, but no sorrow in the voices that uttered and echoed the word—"Dead."

"Yes; she died last Monday."

"Who is the letter from—Eunice?" asked Mrs. Gregory.

"No; it is from Judge Helmbold."

"Ah! How came he to write?"

"I don't know."

"What does he say?"

"He simply mentions the fact that Helen died last Monday, and was interred on Wednesday; and that Eunice is, for the present, at his house."

"At his house!" There was a tone of surprise in the voice of Mrs. Gregory.

"Yes."

"Is she going to stay there?"

"I infer not. Had any such arrangement been made, or in contemplation, the judge would have said so. She is there only temporarily, I infer—that is, until we send for her."

"O dear, pa! you won't do that!" said Harriet, visibly disturbed at this suggestion.

"We don't want her here," added Lizzy, the second daughter.

"We can't have her," said Mrs. Gregory, positively.

"She has no other relatives living," remarked Mr. Gregory, "and it will not look well for us to turn away from the poor orphan. We cannot wholly disregard appearances. She is now at Judge Helmbold's, and it is evident that the judge, out of respect to us, took interest enough in Eunice to give her a home until we could make arrangements to receive her."

"I wish he hadn't meddled himself in the affair," remarked Mrs. Gregory, in no amiable tone of voice. "Eunice is nothing to us."

"She is your brother's child," said her husband, with enough of rebuke in his voice to indicate his better feelings on the subject about which they were talking in such a heartless manner.

"No matter. When he married Helen Leeds he put a distance between us that was never diminished; and when he died I held his widow as a stranger."

Mr. Gregory did not answer to this. He had a kinder heart, and it had been warming toward the motherless girl ever since the reception of Judge Helmbold's letter.

The brother of Mrs. Gregory had married,

in the view of that lady, socially below his family position, and as she was simply a woman of the world, she never gave his wife countenance or favor. His death occurred some years before the period at which our story commences; and now, by the death of his widow, their only child, a daughter in her eighteenth year, was left alone in the world, and penniless. No wonder that a woman like Mrs. Gregory should feel worried at the circumstance. If Judge Helmbold had not received Eunice into his family, nor written to her husband giving information of the sister-in-law's death, the case would have presented a better aspect. Some provision might have been made for the girl in her native place; but now, respect for the good opinion of Judge Helmbold and the circle in which he moved, demanded of them such a recognition of Eunice as would place her side by side with their own daughters. In other words, she must be taken into the family.

Mr. Gregory answered the judge's letter, and enclosed one for Eunice, in which he offered her a home. The letter to Eunice was brief, but kind and sincere. In the course of a week there came a reply from the girl, thanking Mr. Gregory for his tender of a home, and saying that she would be in Boston within a fortnight. She asked to be lovingly remembered to her aunt and cousins, adding that it would have been grateful to her feelings to have received a letter from one of them.

"Harriet," said Mr. Gregory, "you must write to your cousin. It isn't kind!"

"Indeed, pa, you must excuse me," answered the young lady, in a cold, proud manner. "I have nothing to say."

"You could say a kind word to a motherless girl. Think of her lonely, sorrowful condition. It should fill your heart with tenderness and pity."

But Mr. Gregory could make no impression on the proud, unfeeling girl, who was wholly influenced by her mother's estimate of the case.

At the end of a fortnight Eunice arrived.

Mr. Gregory met her at the railway station. He had not seen her for five years, but recognized her in a moment by the large, dark, chestnut brown eyes which he had thought so beautiful in her mother. Her reception, when he presented her at home, was not cordial. The aunt and cousins scarcely veiled their reluctance at receiving her with a decent politeness. They pushed her away from them to the utmost distance in their power, and she moved back, instinctively, at the pressure, and stood afar off—not in tearful submission to her fate, nor in proud defiance—but in such calm, womanly dignity, that her aunt and cousins were embarrassed in their efforts to make up an estimate of her character. She had disappointed them. Her picture, in their minds, had been that of an ordinary looking girl—plain, uninteresting, shrinking—a nobody whom they could snub, and slight, and insult at will. But, instead, Eunice came among them dignified in manner, and impressive in person and bearing. Her face was handsome, rather than plain, and her eyes large, dark, and of that liquid depth which we sometimes see in eyes that appear looking at us from a far distance, and that hold us with a power which we can neither define nor break.

As we said, at the first meeting Mrs. Gregory and her daughters pushed Eunice away from them with a cold repulsion to which her sensitive, but womanly spirit, yielded instantly, and she took her position at such a distance that they were never able to get near her afterward. She was not one to snub, and slight, and insult at will, as they had imagined. O no! There was a tone and an air about her that forbade this. They could be cold and formal, but not insolent—for the calm dignity of her manner, her self-poise, and self-consciousness, repressed rudeness and enforced respect. She never intruded conversation on her aunt and cousins, but often talked with Mr. Gregory when in their presence, in a way to surprise and shame them—the shame being for their own mental inferiority.

As Eunice was in mourning, there was a good reason why she did not see company, and her presence in the Gregory family was scarcely known in their circle of visiting acquaintances. Occasionally she was seen by one and another of their more intimate friends, and when questions were asked in regard to her, she was slightingly referred to as a poor relative to whom they had given a home.

Nearly six months had passed since Eunice came into her uncle's family, and she was almost as much a stranger there as on the day of her entrance. Mr. and Mrs. Gregory were sitting alone one evening, about this time, when Eunice came down from her room and joined them. Mr. Gregory met her with his usual kind manner, Mrs. Gregory with her usual distant politeness. She had, evidently, come with the purpose of talking to them on some matter concerning herself, and she did not keep them waiting.

"For your kindness," she began, with a slight unsteadiness in her voice, which soon grew calm, "in giving me a home up to this time, I shall ever be grateful. I would not have intruded upon you so long, if heart and brain had been strong enough for the work of self-support. Both are strong enough now, I believe, and I have made my arrangements to leave you next week."

"Leave us, Eunice? I don't understand you! For where, and for what?" Mrs. Gregory spoke in real surprise.

"I am going into Miss R——'s school as a teacher," calmly answered the girl.

"No, Eunice," said Mr. Gregory, "you shall do nothing of the kind. You have a home here and welcome. What has possessed you to think of such a thing?"

"I have never intended, Uncle, to burden you with my support," Eunice replied. "Your kind offer of a home I accepted gratefully, while my heart was too heavy with its recent sorrow to bear me out in the world. I am stronger now, and independence is a native element of my character."

"In Miss R——'s school!" exclaimed Mrs.

Gregory, giving voice at length to her astonishment.

"Yes, ma'am," answered Eunice.

'Where Lisette goes?"

"Yes, ma'am."

"No—never!" she said firmly. "I'm not going to have *my* niece a teacher in *that* school. No—nor in any school in Boston."

"Why not?" asked Eunice.

"Is the girl beside herself?"

"You must reconsider this whole matter," said Mr. Gregory. "I'm sorry it was not mentioned before. Have you really engaged with Miss R——?"

"Yes, Sir."

"My niece! Such a disgrace!" ejaculated Mrs. Gregory, carried away by her feelings. "What will be thought of this?"

"I will call on Miss R—— and cancel the engagement," said Mr. Gregory, in the kindest manner. "I regret that you have not felt at home here, but we will try to make things more agreeable. Don't think that you are a burden to us."

"Uncle Gregory," replied Eunice, "I settled this matter long ago. I am too self-reliant and too just, I hope, to live in idle dependence. Since I have been here, I have tried to make myself useful, and to repay your generous kindness in all ways in my power. It has been done inadequately, I know—but the heart of gratitude was there, and it will never cease to beat. Now I go, as I have said."

Remonstrance and persuasion were alike unavailing. At the time specified, Eunice left her uncle's house, and assumed the duties of a teacher in Miss R——'s school, greatly to the scandal and mortification of Mrs. Gregory and her daughters, and greatly to the satisfaction of her own independent mind. The six months she had spent in her uncle's family had been months of painful humiliation, and the time was only prolonged to this period for the reason which has been given.

Among the visiting acquaintances of the Gregorys was a young man named Edmondson. He was a lawyer, whose talents had already attracted public notice, and of whom almost every one predicted a brilliant future. A small fortune had come to him recently, from a distant relative. His talents, person, prospects, and fortune—moderate though it was—gave an aggregate of attractions that made him of no light consideration in the eyes of Mrs. Gregory, who thought him just the man of all others she would like to see the husband of Harriet. In consequence, she was always very gracious to him, and never let a good opportunity for turning his thought toward this daughter pass unimproved. Harriet, in common parlance, was quite in love with him—that is, as much so as was possible for a girl so selfish, worldly, and heartless, to be. He filled her fancy better than any other man she had yet seen. His fortune was not large, but his family was good, and he had talents that were likely to command fortune. Moreover, there were distant relatives possessing large wealth, and the probabilities, it had been reasoned among the Gregorys, were largely in favor of his sharing a portion of this wealth in time.

"Where is that brown-eyed niece of yours, Mrs. Gregory?" asked Mr. Edmondson, one day; "I haven't seen her in some time."

"She is not with us any longer," replied Mrs. Gregory. Her manner told the young man that he had touched a disagreeable subject.

"Ah! I was not aware that she had left you."

Mrs. Gregory said nothing more; but the impression on Mr. Edmondson was unfavorable to Eunice. Sometime afterward, a thought of this girl passing through his mind, he said to a lady with whom he happened to be conversing,

"Did you ever see a young lady in black at Mr. Gregory's?"

"His niece?"

"Yes. A dark-eyed, elegant-looking girl, with something queenly in her manner."

"O, yes. I've met her there occasionally."

"She always seemed to hold herself at a distance."

"That was her manner."

"Was there any thing wrong about her?"

"Why do you ask?"

"I inferred as much, from the aspect of Mrs. Gregory, when I inquired about her not long ago."

"Ah! Then you asked after her? What reply did you receive?"

"The unsatisfactory one, that she did not reside with them any longer. From her manner, I inferred that there was something wrong about the young lady."

"Would you like to know of that something wrong?"

"It gives me no pleasure to hear wrong of any one: but, in the few times that I saw her, the girl interested me, and I would, therefore, like to know the truth in regard to her."

"She left the house of her uncle and aunt, to become a teacher in Miss R——'s school," said the lady.

"Why so?"

"Because she had too much spirit to eat the bread of dependence."

"Is that so?" There was a quick lighting up of Mr. Edmondson's face.

"Even so."

"And is there nothing wrong beyond this?"

"Nothing that I have heard. Against her purity of character, slander, I take it, dare not even whisper. And Miss R—— says, that in sweetness of temper, womanly dignity, self-reliance, and Christian patience in the discharge of duty, she is peerless."

"I like all that!" replied the young man, with enthusiasm. "Here we have a real woman; not a weak, selfish, proud, indolent, spoiled nursling of a luxurious home, reared by as weak and selfish a mother, and kept in laces and satins, and pillowed on down, for some silly man who is weak enough to take her in the hope of getting a wife! Of what use to any one in this world of care, sorrow, trial, reverses, and disappointments, is a silly doll like that? He is a fool, who tries the voyage of life with such a helpless companion. I pity him when the sky darkens, and the storms fall! The niece, I infer, was poor."

"Yes. A brother of Mrs. Gregory married a girl whose position in life did not suit her high notions; and so neither himself nor wife had any countenance. The brother died some years ago, and his widow, and true, good woman, as I have learned, struggled alone with poverty, to raise and educate her daughter. She died, after well accomplishing her work. The Gregorys then offered Eunice a home. They were written to, I believe, by Judge Helmbold, of Windham; and she was taken into their family, as I infer, merely to save appearances."

"Why, a girl like this one is worth a hundred idle fashionables!" said Mr. Edmondson. "I must know her."

"Win her and wear her, if you can, my young friend," said the lady. "But such as she are not lightly won. Fruit of this quality does not hang low, but on the higher branches; and they who pluck it must climb."

"Thank you for the hint," replied the young man. "I will climb."

A few months afterward, Mrs. Gregory received this note from Miss R——:

"DEAR MADAM: I think it is my duty to inform you that a gentleman, Mr. Harvey Edmondson, is in the habit of visiting your niece frequently; and they are often out together in the evening. I have spoken to her once or twice on the subject, but have not received answers that were altogether satisfactory. I have every confidence in her as a pure, good girl; and yet, as I cannot feel sure of Mr. Edmondson's honorable intentions, I am naturally concerned. As her nearest relative, I think it best that you should be advised of the facts as they exist."

There was considerable stir among the Gregorys, on receipt of this letter. The worst was inferred by all; no, not by all, for Mr. Gregory's thought went first to the truth, though it wavered a little under the positive conclusions of his wife. What was to be done? With Eunice, they could have no influence; for, since the step which had made her a teacher, instead of an idle dependent, there had been no intercourse between them. As a mere teacher, she could not be received by them as an equal and friend, and she would not meet them on any other footing. So, she could not be admonished or controlled. The only mode of interference suggested was that of Mr. Gregory, as directed upon the young man himself. Mrs. Gregory insisted upon it, that her husband should caution the young lawyer against any further advance in that direction. She remembered how she had herself given Mr. Edmondson the impression there was something wrong about Eunice; and now conscience—no, a dread of family disgrace in the person of her niece—troubled her considerably. It was plain to her, that she had herself put the destroyer on the track of her niece.

"Have you seen Mr. Edmondson yet?" she

asked, almost daily, of her husband. But Mr. Gregory, whose anxieties on the subject had never been very disturbing, invariably said no.

About this time, cards of invitation were received from a family of high social standing in the city—a family whose position was not based on wealth, but on something harder to acquire, and more enduring. The Gregorys were flattered by the notice taken of them in this invitation, and were at special pains, like all vulgar people, to make an imposing appearance on the occasion.

The company was not large, but select; and, certainly, Mrs. Gregory and her two daughters did make an appearance. There was no such display of costly laces and jewels in the room. The guests were in two large parlors, opening into each other by folding doors. Soon after the arrival of the Gregorys, Mr. Edmondson moved through the room in which they sat, and seeing them, joined their circle. There was nothing of coldness or reserve on the part of Mrs. Gregory or her daughters, toward the man whose apparent relation with respect to their niece and cousin, was of a questionable character, but, a fluttering pleasure that was not concealed. No one who saw the smiles with which he was received, and the pleased affability that was maintained, could have imagined how the case really stood.

Mr. Edmondson was still talking with the Gregorys, when a movement indicated a selection of partners for dancing. The young man, instead of asking Harriet to take a place with him on the floor, merely bowed and withdrew. In a little while, gay music filled the air, and beauty wheeled in intervolving circles through the rooms. No one offered a hand to either of the Miss Gregorys, and they sat, in some disappointment, where they had taken their places, on entering the parlors. Mr. Edmondson was on the floor, in the other room, but they were not, at first, from their position, able to make out his partner, of whom they could only get fleeting glimpses, as she swept to the outer circles in the mazy figures. They saw that she was tall, beautifully formed, and graceful in her movements, but attired with exceeding plainness. Her face did not happen to be toward them, when her person was seen.

Who was she? That was the one question in their thoughts. The solution came. As the figures took a reverse motion, the faces of the dancers were seen successively, and that of Mr. Edmondson's partner was presented to the eyes of Mrs. Gregory and her daughters, radiant with beauty and feeling.

"What a sweet, pure, lovely face it is," remarked a lady, who had seen the countenance of Mr. Edmondson's partner. She addressed Mrs. Gregory, but received no response. If she had looked closely, she would have noticed a sickly pallor on her face.

"His *fiancé*, I believe," said another lady, turning to the one who had spoken.

"Ah! Is that so?" With some interest.

"Yes; and I admire the manly independence which has determined his choice."

"Why so? It strikes me, judging from the countenance I saw just now, that manly independence could have very little to do with the selection."

"And I presume had not; but we are apt to speak after this fashion, when a young man in his position and with his prospects, selects a poor girl for his life companion—one standing quite alone in the world, and self-dependent."

"And this is her case?"

"Yes."

"Who is she?"

"A Miss Hadley."

"What of her?"

"She is a teacher in Miss R——'s school."

"Ah!"

"Yes;—and I am told that she chose the life of a teacher, in preference to idle dependence on wealthy relatives who offered her a home."

"Noble girl! I like that!" was the warm-spoken response. "The true woman proved itself there. Our young friend showed good sense, as well as good taste. But, who are these relatives? Do they live in Boston?"

"Yes; but I have not heard their names. They are, as I understand, rich nobodies, who offered her a home to save appearances, but who never countenanced her after she elected independence and a teacher's life."

"And Mr. Edmondson is really going to marry her?"

"O, yes. That is all settled, I hear."

"Then I shall claim her as a friend. Give me the womanly quality, and I will let others content themselves with the effigies of women, elaborately made up, that flutter in our social circles like butterflies, and who are about as substantial as these aerial beings. Money will give you such creatures by the hundred; but solid substance-women are of rarer production."

The Gregorys heard no more, for the two ladies arose and went to another part of the room. But that was quite enough to make their pride, vanity, and poor self-estimation as limp as a wet ribbon. It was as the lady had said. Eunice had become the affianced of Mr. Edmondson ; and it was in recognition of this, that she was the guest, on that evening, of a lady whose social position was among the first in Boston ; and when, in a few months afterward, she became a bride, she passed into a circle of refinement and intelligence that never opened, except specially and in cold formality, to mere outside people like her aunt and cousins.

IX.

THE GREAT MAN.

It happened, once upon a time, that in a certain manufacturing town, the location of which need not be indicated, a movement, humanitarian in its object, was initiated by three or four right-minded individuals who did not happen to possess any of the usually required elements of influence. That is, they were poor young men, occupying humble positions, and scarcely known beyond a very limited circle in their own neighborhood.

These young men had observed with concern, the neglected condition of a large number of children whose parents were employed from ten to twelve hours in the factories every day. Only a few of them attended school, and these were constantly tempted by the others to absent themselves and join in their depraving sports. More than a hundred of such children, boys and girls, were growing up idle and vicious; and nobody seemed to care for them. Pests of the neighborhood, they were execrated, but not pitied with that true human pity which seeks to reform and save.

The young men to whom we have referred, talked frequently together on the subject of these unfortunate children, and at last resolved to make an effort in their behalf, with the townspeople. But, they lacked, as we have said, the usually required elements of influence. Some listened with cold politeness; some with but half concealed impatience; some with a quick rejection, so far as they were concerned, of all interest in the matter; a few spoke in commiseration—but all discouragingly.

"Let us call a public meeting at the Court-House," suggested one of the more earnest ot the young men, "and put the matter fairly before our citizens." Acting on the suggestion, the use of the Court-House was obtained for a certain evening. The next thing was to secure an attendance.

There was in the town a lawyer of splendid abilities named Thurlow. He had the gift of language in a remarkable degree, and could hold almost any audience entranced by the power of his commanding eloquence. Mr. Thurlow was a very ambitious man. He looked forward to the attainment of a high place in the nation. Already he had been sent to the Legislature of his State twice; and now his thoughts were turned upon Congress. Mr. Thurlow was a shrewd, far-seeing, prudent man—so far as mere human prudence goes—and never did any thing from sudden impulse; or, as it is said, on the spur of the moment. There was in the world only one man for whom he cared any thing, and that was himself. So action was always preceded by the thought, "How will this affect my standing and prospects!" True honor, in his estimation, was a high place among the distinguished and powerful. As he rose, by means of his fine talents and power, to sway men through the magic of voice and words, his bearing grew more erect, and his manner more self-conscious. From the "common herd," he held himself more aloof; not in an offensive way, for he was a political aspirant, and that would have been fatal to his ambitious hopes—he must stoop to conquer here. But, he held himself aloof, while seeming in contact, as oil keeps free from water. He might float on the waves, but never mingle with them. He might use the lower stratum of society as a means of elevation, while yet despising them as inferior.

Such, in brief, was Mr. Thurlow; and to him the thought of our young humanitarians turned. He was waited on by two of the young men. They were strangers to him, and in appearance, manner and address, showed themselves to be from the humble walks of life. He heard them respectfully, and then answered:

"This is a matter of too light importance for me to engage in, my young friends. Get clergymen to help in the work you have undertaken. The field is more legitimately theirs than ours."

"You can help more than any other man in town," was urged. "Only let us announce you as a speaker, and the court-room will be crowded. And only give your hearty approval, backed by such an appeal as you can make, and a hundred neglected children may be saved from vice, idleness and crime."

But Mr. Thurlow shook his head, answering,

"I must beg to be excused, gentlemen. Your choice of me is flattering, but I can't address your meeting. And permit me to suggest," he added, with his bland, worldly smile, "that you are looking, perhaps, a little too high in your choice of influencing means. Humble work, like yours, away down in the very lowest places of life, is done by the humbler agencies. Take them, my young friends, and operate by them. Excuse me for saying this; but the hint will be of use. It is given in all courtesy."

And Mr. Thurlow bowed the young men out. They walked away in silence and discouragement.

"Shall the poor, neglected, almost off-cast children of the poor—God's poor—find no advocate with the people?" said one of the young men, speaking at last, and with some bitterness. "My heart aches under its burden of helplessness. How little can we do without a general countenance and co-operation of the citizens; yet how are we to secure this? One hour given to the cause by Mr. Thurlow, would have effected more than we can ever hope to accomplish. And yet, in his imagined greatness, he stands so far above the work that he cannot touch it with a finger. Alas, for such greatness! It is of self and for self; and selfishness is always mean and little in spirit, no matter what outside importance it may reach by inflation. Mr. Thurlow may go on rising; but he can never be a truly great man."

In the evening of that day, the young men met again to confer together on the subject near their hearts.

"Mr. W—— arrived in town to-day," remarked one of them.

"So I heard. Ah, if we could only get him to address our meeting!"

"Yes; that would settle the question," was replied. "But such a thing is not, of course, to be thought of."

"No. What power resides in talent! If it would now and then step aside from its ambitious paths, and stay its onward march to greatness, in order to help the weak, succor the oppressed, and teach the ignorant, what noble things for humanity might be accomplished!"

Mr. W—— was among the nation's most distinguished men. He had been for years in public life, and had occupied the highest positions in the country, next to the Presidency. His oratory was splendid.

Yes, if they could get Mr. W—— to address their meeting, their work would be of certain accomplishment. It came, at length, into the most sanguine of the party's thought, to approach Mr. W—— on the subject. His heart so yearned for the poor children, and he felt so deeply his own want of power and influence, that he was like a man in danger grappling around him with something of desperation, and seizing upon the strong for support. So he called, alone, upon Mr. W——. He found two or three gentlemen with him; the town's best people, so called; and so esteemed, at least by themselves. Mr. Thurlow was of the number. He recognized our young philanthropist, and frowned as a suspicion of the truth crossed his mind.

"What do you want with Mr. W——?" he asked, in an undertone, as he crossed the room quickly, and met him ere he had moved three steps from the door of the entrance. Mr. Thurlow felt in duty bound to save the great man from unwarrantable intrusion and annoyance.

"I wish to speak a word with him," answered the young man, in firm but respectful voice.

"Not about those dirty little vagabonds over by the mills?" Mr. Thurlow's manner was excited.

"Yes, Sir, about those dirty little vagabonds over by the mills, as you are pleased to call them," said the young man, a feeling of indignation against the lawyer coming in at the right moment to give his mind firmness and tone. His heart beat falteringly as he came in, but now he felt brave. Mr. Thurlow, in attempting to place an impediment in his way, had only developed native force.

"You can't speak with him on that subject," said Mr. Thurlow. "I will protect him from such impertinence. It is disgraceful!"

Of course, this aside interview attracted Mr. W——'s attention. Though he did not hear, distinctly, what was said, he understood that the young man had called to see him, and stepping forward, he said, in a kind way—

"What is it? Does the gentleman wish to speak with me?"

"I came for that purpose," answered the young man, "and will consider it a great favor if you will let me say a few words. I am sure you will listen to me with interest."

Mr. W—— was impressed favorably. He

saw true manhood, and the signs of a right purpose in the visitor, humble though he was in exterior compared to the elaborately made-up lawyer. And he answered with blandness and encouragement.

"I have no doubt of it in the world. Come, sit down, and say as many words as you please."

Mr. Thurlow stepped aside as the young man advanced towards Mr. W——, muttering half aloud—

"Too bad! Too bad! The fellow should be horsewhipped!"

Mr. W—— heard the last sentence; he felt surprise, but no abatement of interest. Something in the visitor had won him. His true perceptions had penetrated below the surface, and recognized the stamp of genuine manhood, and with that he was in sympathy, everywhere and at all times.

"Sit down, Sir." Mr. W—— pointed to a chair. The young man sat down, and Mr. W——, taking a seat near him, put on the aspect of a listener. Mr. Thurlow, indignant, outraged, but silent, walked the room uneasily. He felt that this intrusion was a disgrace to their town. To have a parcel of ragged, dirty children thrust offensively under the great man's nose. It was shocking. Every moment he expected to see Mr. W—— start to his feet, and tower upward angrily, like a full-charged thunder-cloud. He did not hear what the visitor said ; no, he was too much excited even to listen. The young man talked earnestly for several minutes. Then there was a pause. Mr. W—— was about to speak. The indignant lawyer listened for the words.

"When is the meeting to be held?" There was a touch of feeling in Mr. W——'s voice. Mr. Thurlow was in doubt whether his sense of hearing were not at fault.

"We have the Court-House for Thursday evening," said the young man.

"And this is Monday." Mr. W—— looked thougthful and a little in doubt. "My intention was to leave on to-morrow afternoon."

"Don't think of this thing, sir!" exclaimed Mr. Thurlow, coming forward and speaking with indignant warmth. "It's an outrage! I call it by no better name. The impudence of the application is only exceeded by its absurdity. The idea of your making an address in behalf of a parcel of miserable factory children! Our citizens have no hand in this affair, Sir. They will be angry at the insult when the fact becomes known. You'd better retire, Sir!" looking at the young man, and waving his hand towards the door.

"It is God's cause," said the young man, rising; his manner was dignified; his voice calm, clear, and full of that eloquence which the heart gives; "and His cause is always noblest and best. Oh, Sir!"—his eager face was turned full upon Mr. W——, "if you can linger here for one day, and give to this work a single hour, you will set on foot good impulses the fruit of which can never die. A hundred children rescued from ignorance and vice—the nursing mothers of crime—through one hour's earnest turning of the people's thought to duty by the power of that noble eloquence with which the Father of us all has endowed you!

It is not mean, debasing work, Sir ; but great and good work. It will not be coming down, Sir ; but going up, and standing side by side with angels."

"Thanks, my young friend," said Mr. W——, with emotion, as he took the earnest speaker's hand, "for all you have said and urged. I will remain over until Thursday, and plead for this good cause ; and it shall not be stayed for any lack of effort on my part. Call your meeting, and announce me for the occasion. At twelve to-morrow see me here, and give me all the facts I shall need. Good day, Sir! Count on my services, and in the strength of God I will not fail you!"

"And God will give strength and a reward," answered the young man, as he held Mr. W——'s hand, and looked up at him with a glad face and tear-brimming eyes; then he turned and left the apartment.

The large court-room would not hold one half of the eager citizens who pressed for entrance on Thursday evening. Mr. W—— met them, with his great, true heart in the cause he had tarried to plead. The conduct of Mr. Thurlow had acted as an incentive in the right direction. He looked through the little selfishness of the would-be great man, and despised him.

When the heart of such a man as Mr. W—— melts to his theme, eloquence becomes irresistible. He took up the poor children, as in a tableaux, and presented them to his audience in such distinctness of aspect that shame, pity, and right resolve filled every breast. Then he spoke of them as living souls, each heaven-born and immortal; and in a few strong sentences showed the wonderful beauty, power, and nobleness of a human soul, compared with which man's highest works were mean and insignificant.

"If the Great God himself," he said, in a low, hushed, reverent voice, that went thrilling with its deep pathos to every heart in the assembly, "came down, stooping even to the assumption of our debased and depraved human souls, can we do a nobler work than now presents itself? Can we be more honored than to stand side by side with Him? I feel, at this moment, that I am pleading the greatest cause that has ever claimed my advocacy—the cause of human souls; weak, unguarded, almost helpless human souls, for the destruction of which all hell is moving. O, friends of humanity!" his voice broke out like a trumpet call—"to the rescue! to the rescue!"

When he sat down there needed no second advocate. A meeting was organized on the spot, and the wealthiest and most influential citizens moved to the work before them as with the will of a single man. Funds were subscribed liberally, and a committee appointed to organize a school, and to adopt all right means for attaining the end proposed.

As Mr. W—— moved amid the crowd, on his way to the door, after all was over, a hand caught one of his hands in a close, eager grasp, and a low voice said in his ears:

"God will remember you for this, in the day of his coming."

"And he will remember you also," was the reply of Mr. W——, as he recognized the young man who had moved him to the good work, and returned the warm pressure of his hand. They parted there, and never met again; but the single hour which that giant among his fellows gave to humanity, was productive of results that will live in still higher achievements, through ages yet unborn. Who can tell what good and great things for the world may flow from the action of one human soul, rescued from ignorance and evil?

If our great men—our men who by talent, wealth, distinction, or soul-stirring eloquence, have power to move the people, would step down occasionally from their high places, and seek to elevate the low, enlighten the ignorant, and save the vicious, what a new impulse to all humanitarian movements would be awakened. No man who goes down, in order to lift up the weak, the helpless, the fallen and degraded, loses any thing of his true dignity.

Far from it! In the sight of good men and angels, he towers far above the crowd of mean, self-aggrandizers, who would stand even on the necks of the fallen, in order to lift themselves into public observation. Truly noble work is unselfish work; and he is the noblest man who is least selfish. There is no higher patent of nobility than this. It is registered in heaven, "Whosoever would be chief among you, let him be your servant."

X.

A TALK ABOUT MARRIAGE.

Two maidens, in youthful bloom and beauty, sat earnestly talking. Their thought was reaching away into the future; their theme was marriage.

"I like him well enough," said one of them; "but—"

She paused, the objection unspoken.

"What is the impediment, Alice?"

"His income is too small."

"What is it?"

"Eight hundred dollars a year."

"You might live on that."

"Live! Bah! What kind of living?"

"Not in princely style, I will admit."

"Nor scarcely in plebeian, Fanny. Eight hundred dollars! Why, father pays six hundred dollars rent; and I'm sure our style of living is plain enough! Eight hundred! Oh no. I like Harry better than any young man I have met. I could love him, no doubt. But he can't support a wife in any decent kind of style."

"Did your father and mother begin their married life on a larger income than Harry Plesants now receives? Mine did not, as I have often heard them relate."

"Father and mother! Oh, according to their story, Job's famous turkey was scarcely poorer than they were in the beginning. Mother did all her own work, even to the washing and ironing, I believe. Father's income was not over three or four hundred dollars a year."

"And they were happy together, I am sure."

"No doubt. In fact, I've heard mother say, that the first hard struggling years of their life, were among the happiest she has known. But that doesn't signify for me. That is no reason why her daughter should elect to go into the kitchen, and spend her years in washing, ironing and cooking. If a man isn't able to support a wife genteelly, and in the style to which she has been accustomed, let him marry some Irish cook, sewing girl, or washerwoman, who will manage his household with the needed economy. Young men who can't earn more than eight hundred or a thousand dollars a year, should not look into our circle for wives."

"I don't like to hear you talk in this way, Alice," said her companion. "We are not superior beings, but only the equals of men."

"Did I say that we were superior?"

"One might infer from your language that you thought so."

"I don't see how the inference can fairly be drawn."

"*Our* circle for wives, you said just now."

"Yes."

"What do you mean by it?"

"A circle of intelligence, refinement, taste and cultivation," replied Alice.

"You don't say wealth."

"No. My father, though living in good

style, is not rich. I have heard him say, more than once, that we were up to our income."

"Then, we have only our own sweet selves with which to endow our husbands. No houses, or lands; no stocks from which to draw an income; nothing substantial on which to claim the right of being supported in costly idleness. We must be rich indeed, as to personal attractions."

"We are educated, accomplished, and—and—"

Alice was a little bewildered in thought, and did not finish the sentence.

"Not better educated, or accomplished, as girls, than are most of the young men who, as clerks, earn only from seven hundred to a thousand dollars a year. In this regard, we are simply their equals. But it strikes me, that, in another view of the case we cannot claim even an equality. They are our superiors."

"Not by any means," replied Alice.

"We shall see. Here is Harry Pleasants,

for instance. What is his income? I think you mentioned the sum just now."

"Eight hundred dollars a year."

"That is the interest on—how much?—let me see—about twelve thousand dollars. To be equal, as a match for Harry, then, you should be worth twelve thousand dollars."

"How you talk, Fanny!"

"To the point, don't I? If we are not superior to the young men who visit us; superior simply in virtue of our sex; then, our only claim to be handsomely supported in idle self-indulgence, must lie in the fact, that we endow our husbands with sufficient worldly goods to warrant the condition."

"You are ingenious."

"No, matter-of-fact. What have you to say against my position, Alice? Are we better than young men of equal intelligence and education?"

"No; I cannot say that we are."

"If we marry, we must look among these for husbands. Rich men, as a general thing, select their wives from rich men's daughters.

Our chances in that direction are not very encouraging. Your father has no dowry for his child; nor has mine. Their families are large and expensive, and little or nothing of the year's income is left at the year's close. The best they can do for us, is to give us homes; and I feel that it is not much to our credit that we are content to lean on our fathers, already stooping under the burdens of years, care and toil, instead of supporting ourselves. The thought has troubled me, of late."

A sober hue came over the face of Alice, as she sat looking into the eyes of her friend. She did not reply, and Fanny went on.

"There is wrong in this. On what ground of reason are we to be exempt from the common lot of useful work? We expect to become wives and mothers. Is this our preparation? Can you bake a loaf of sweet, light bread!"

"No."

"Nor can I. Or roast a sirlion?"

"No."

"Or broil a steak? Just think of it, Alice! We can manage a little useless embroidery, or fancy knitting; can sing and play, dance and chatter—but as to the real and substantial things of life, we are ignorant and helpless. And, with all this, forsooth, we cannot think of letting ourselves down to the level and condition of virtuous, intelligent young men, who, in daily, useful work, are earning fair indepenence! We are so superior that we must have husbands able to support us in luxurious idleness, or we will have none! We are willing to pass the man to whom love would unite us in the tenderest bonds, because his income is small, and marry for position, one from whom the soul turns with instinctive aversion. Can we wonder that so many are unhappy?"

"But eight hundred dollars, Fanny! How is it possible for a married couple to live in any decent style, in this city, on eight hundred dollars a year?"

"They may live in a very comfortable style, if the wife is willing to perform her part."

"What do you mean by her part, Fanny?"

"We will take it for granted, that she is no better than her husband. That, having brought him no fortune beyond her own dear self, she cannot claim superior privileges."

"Well?"

"He has to work through all the day."

"Well?"

"Under what equitable rule is she exempt?"

"None. She must do her part, of course, if there is any thing to do with. She must keep his house, if he can afford a house. But if he have only eight hundred dollars a year! Why, rent alone would consume half, or more than half of that. There would be no house-keeping in the case. They must board."

"And the wife sit in idleness all day long?"

"She would have nothing to do."

"Could she not teach? or, by aid of a sewing machine, earn a few dollars every week? or engage in some other useful work that would yield an income; and so do her part?"

"Yes, she *might* do something of the kind;

but if marriage is to make 'workies' of us, it were better to remain single."

"And live in unwomanly dependence on our parents or relatives. No, Alice; there is a false sentiment prevailing on this subject, and as I think and talk, I see it more and more clearly. Our parents have been weak in their love for us; and society, as constituted, has given us wrong estimates of things. We should have been required to do useful work in the household, from the beginning; and should have been taught that idleness and self indulgence were discreditable. Our brothers are put to trades and professions, and made to comprehend, from the beginning, that industry is honorable, and that the way of useful work is the way by which the world's brightest places are to be reached. But we are raised daintily and uselessly, and so fitted for our duties as wives and mothers. Our pride and self-esteem are fostered; and we come to think of ourselves as future queens, who are to be ministered to in all things, instead of being ministrant, in loving self-forgetfulness, to others. No wonder that an anti-marriage sentiment is beginning to prevail amongst young men of moderate incomes, in all our large cities. The fault is in us, Alice. The sin lies at our door. We demand too much in the copartnership. We are not willing to do our share of work. Our husbands must bear all the burdens."

Alice sighed heavily. Her friend continued:

"I have read somewhere that the delight of heaven is the delight of being useful. And it seems to me, as I dwell upon the thought, that the nearest approach to heavenly delight here, must be that state into which a wife comes when she stands by her husband's side, and, out of love for him, removes one burden and another from his shoulders, and so lightens his work that smiles take the place of weariness and the shadowings of care. If he be rich, she can hardly have so great a privilege; but if they are alike poor, and know how to moderate their desires, their home may become an image of paradise.

Eight hundred dollars! Alice, if you were really fitted to become Harry's wife, you might live with him, doing your part, happier than any queen.

"That is, I must take in work, and earn money, if we board: or—but housekeeping is out of the question."

"No; it should never be out the question in marriage, I think."

"But house-rent alone would take half of our income."

"That does not follow."

"It does, for any house I would consent to live in."

"So pride is stronger than love. But pride has its wages as well as love; and the one is bitter while the other is sweet. It is this pride of appearance, this living for the eyes of other people who do not care a penny for us, that is marring the fair fabric of our social life. Fine houses, fine furniture, fine dresses, parties, shows and costly luxuries of all kinds, are consuming domestic happiness, and burdening fathers and husbands, in all grades of society, with embarrassment and wretchedness. Alice, we must be wiser in our generation."

"That is, coop ourselves up in two or three mean little rooms, with our eight hundred dollars a year husbands, and do our own cooking and housework. Is that it, my pretty one?"

"For shame, Alice! You do not deserve a good man. You are not worthy to wed Harry Pleasants, and I trust you will pass him by, should he be weak enough to offer you his hand. He can't afford to marry a girl of your expectations; he must content himself with one who, like himself, regards life as real, life as earnest; and the way of use and duty the way to true honor and the highest happiness."

"Suppose you take him, Fanny," said Alice, half sportively, half petulantly. She was a weak, proud, vain girl.

"If he should offer himself, perhaps I will."

"Oh, then, if he kneels at my feet, I will

refer him to you as one likely to make him a good cook and chambermaid."

"Do, if you please. I always liked Harry, and I don't think it would take much effort on my part to love him. He is a great deal better in the world than I am, having an income of eight hundred dollars a year, while I have nothing. On that sum, I am sure, we could live in comfort, taste, and happiness. I would not keep a servant to wait on me so long as I could do the work of our little household. Why should I keep a servant any more than he? I would find mental recreation and bodily health in the light tasks our modest home would require? Need we care as to what the world would say? And what would the world say?"

"That your husband had no business to marry if he couldn't support his wife!"

"Not by any means, Alice. The world would say, 'There's a sensible couple for you, and a wife worth having. We'll indorse them for happiness and prosperity.' And, what is more, Alice, others would be encouraged to act the same wise part, and thus be made happy through our example. I'll take Harry if he offers himself, and show you a model home and a model wife; so pass him over to me, should he lay his fortune at your feet."

XI.

WORDS FITLY SPOKEN.

"HAVE you called to see Mr. Parsons?" asked Mrs. Fuller, addressing her husband.

"Not yet. The fact is, I feel rather diffident about going to see him. If I could help him; if I had any suggestions to make, or any thing to offer him, it would be different. But his trouble is beyond my ability to reach. Some men are peculiarly sensitive when things go wrong with them. I know how it is with myself. He might consider my visit an intrusion."

Mrs. Fuller thought differently. She did not see the case from her husband's point of view.

"Most people," she replied, "are grateful for any manifested interest in time of grief or trouble, if it be sincere. They easily discriminate between curious intrusion and genuine good feeling."

"Very true," answered Mr. Fuller. "But a man in Mr. Parsons's condition wants something more than sympathy. He wants help."

"Perhaps you can help him," said Mrs. Fuller.

"Me?" The surprise of Mr. Fuller was unfeigned.

"Help comes by many ways. You may be able to suggest the very thing he needs."

"To a man who has been living for the last ten years at an expense three or four times greater than my whole income! O, no! I can't help him. If I had ten thousand dollars to spare, there would be some sense in my calling."

But Mrs. Fuller did not see it in this light.

"Self-help is the surest help," she returned. "A quick, suggestive mind, may get more of the true material of prosperity from a hint than from thousands of dollars."

"Not from any hint of mine. It's of no use for you to argue with me in that direction," said the husband. "Parsons can teach me twenty things where I can teach him one."

"And your one may be of more use to him than his twenty to you," said Mrs. Fuller.

The woman saw that she was right, and did not yield. Will is very persevering. After tea—for it was in the evening—Mrs. Fuller drifted upon the subject of their unfortunate neighbor again, and insisted that it was her husband's duty to make him a call.

"If I could see any use in it," answered Mr. Fuller. "If I had any suggestions to make that would be of value to him."

"It will be of use for him to know that you have not forgotten an old friend and neighbor," replied Mrs. Fuller. "There will be enough to recede—to stand afar off—to look on him coldly, or to pass him by as of but small account to the world, seeing that he no longer has the old money value."

In the end, Mrs. Fuller prevailed. Her husband, after concluding to make the visit, thought he would defer it until the next evening; but she urged that the present hour for a kind act was the best hour.

It was after eight o'clock when Fuller stood

at Mr. Parsons's door. He felt sure that his visit would be considered an intrusion, if not an impertinence. That Mr. Parsons would see in it a rude intimation that they were now on the same social level. His hand grasped the bell, but he hesitated to ring. If the thought of his wife, and what she would say if he went home without accomplishing the errand that took him out, had not crossed his mind, he would have turned away from the door. But that thought stimulated his wavering purpose, and the bell was rung.

A servant showed him into the library, where he found Mr. Parsons alone. He had anticipated a cold and formal reception—he was prepared for it; but not for the light of pleasure that beamed in Mr. Parsons's countenance, nor for the cordial hand-clasp with which he was received.

The two men sat down by the library table, on which were packages of letters, accounts, legal papers, and other evidences going to show that Mr. Parsons had business on hand when his visitor called.

"I fear this may be an interruption," said Mr. Fuller glancing at the table.

"No, your coming is welcome and timely. I was just wishing for a cool, clear-seeing, conscientious friend with whom to take counsel; and I believe you are the man. You know that I am in trouble?"

"Yes."

"The failure of Lawrence & James involves every thing I have. I am on their paper for more than I am worth."

"But they will have assets. The loss will not be complete."

"In the mean time, being under protest on their paper, my credit is gone. The banks throw me out, and I can only get money on the street at ruinous rates. To struggle longer would be folly. Usurers would get what creditors might divide. To-day my own bills went into the Notary's hand."

"So I have heard."

"Such news flies through business circles with electric swiftness. Well, the agony is over; the dread trial past. My name, as drawer, is dishonored—I am a broken merchant."

His voice expressed bitterness of feeling.

"Commercial dishonor is one thing—personal dishonor another," said Mr. Fuller.

Mr. Parsons looked away from the face of his visitor. He moved with a slight gesture of uneasiness—a shade went over his countenance.

"Men who go down into the valley of misfortune," added Mr. Fuller, "tread on slippery ground. They must look well to their feet."

There was no response to this.

"On safer ground," continued Mr. Fuller, "we may recover a false step; but here it is very difficult; sometimes impossible. We are no longer masters of the situation. It will not do to risk any thing."

Still Mr. Parsons remained silent with his face turned partly away.

"All doubtful expedients should be avoided," Mr. Fuller went on, following out the train of thought which had been suggested to his mind. "They are never safe, under the most favorable circumstances; but when misfortune limits and cripples a man, they almost always fail, and leave him more unhappily situated than before."

"Unquestionably you are right," said Mr. Parsons, taking a deep breath. He spoke partly to himself. From his tone, it was plain that he was thinking intently. "When a man gets into trouble," he added, "it is of the first importance to him to show a clear record. As the case now stands, I think mine is clear. I will be misjudged, no doubt. All men are who fail in business. The first impression is against them. How ready the tongue is to whisper, 'There's something wrong!' It is difficult for certain men, when they lose their money, to believe in any thing but roguery."

"Being rogues at heart themselves," said Mr. Fuller.

"No; that does not always follow. I have known some very honest men to be severe on their debtors, and quick to judge them harshly."

"Did you ever see these 'honest' men tried in the crucible of misfortune? Did you ever see them amidst their falling fortunes—bewildered, half blind, grappling this way and that for help, like drowning men?"

"I cannot now recall an instance," said Mr. Parsons.

"I can," replied his visitor—"many instances; and the clear record of which you speak did not always appear when the struggle was over."

Mr. Parsons sighed heavily.

"These are difficult waters to navigate," he remarked, in a tone of sadness, not unmingled with doubt and perplexity. "The man is in danger."

"Of losing his integrity."

"Yes; in great danger."

"With honor at the helm, and rectitude for pilot, the passage is safe."

"And faith in God!" said Mr. Parsons. speaking as from a sudden impulse. His countenance lighted up; his eyes grew calm and steady.

"Yes, faith in God always," replied Mr. Fuller. "He is very near to us, especially in trouble; and if we decide to do right, he will show us what is right. We must not hesitate to put our trust in him. No matter how dark it may be; no matter how many lions are in the path of duty, our safest way is right onward. If we turn aside our souls are in peril."

After sitting with Mr. Parsons for an hour, Mr. Fuller went home. Their conversation had been of the general character we have seen, touching mainly on those principles that lie at the basis of all right actions.

"It was kind in you to call," said the former, as his visitor retired. "I think you have helped me to see some things in a strong light that were obscure before. It is often very dark with men so hard-pressed as I am—with men who grope amid the ruins of a falling fortune. Friendly counsel is good for them. Come and see me again."

It was, perhaps, a month later that Mr. Fuller, urged once more by his wife, called upon Mr. Parsons. He was one of your diffident, retiring men, who are always afraid of intruding themselves. His wife, who knew his worth as a man, and understood his true value among men, was always disposed to push him out of himself, and farther into the social circle than he was inclined, of his own accord, to go.

"Ah, Mr. Fuller! I am glad to see you! Why have you not called before?" was the warm greeting he received. Mr. Parsons still had a care-worn look, but his manner was more cheerful and confident.

"I have had it on my thought many times; but I did not wish to intrude myself."

"Your calls can never be regarded as intrusions, Mr. Fuller," was replied, with much earnestness of manner. "No, never," was added. "I think your visit, one month ago, at a time when I was in great darkness and bewilderment, was a direct interposition of Providence. When you called, I was deeply revolving a scheme that promised extrication. It was not a very safe scheme; it was hardly just—nay, it was not just, for, if it had failed, it would have involved in loss persons in no way concerned in my affairs at the time. That it must have failed, is now clear to me, and I should not only have hurt myself inwardly, but given fair cause for a harsh judgment. But to-day, Mr. Fuller, I bear a clear conscience. I am right with myseif, and can look every man I meet fairly in the face. I have thanked you, a hundred times, for your fitly spoken words. They were as apples of gold in pictures of silver."

"And yet I came with great reluctance, fear ing to intrude," said Mr. Fuller.

"If we mean kindly, we shall rarely intrude," was answered. "When we get in trouble, our friends and neighbors are too apt to recede from us; not from lack of interest or sympathy, I am sure, but from a false impression that we are sullen, morose, or full of sensitive pride, and will repel advances. But it is not so. Misfortune sweeps off a great deal of pride, and mellows the harvest. There are few men in trouble who will consider the call of an old friend or acquaintance as untimely.

Thousands, I am persuaded, might be saved from false steps if their friends would come close about them and help them to find the right path for their straying and stumbling feet. In the multitude of counsellors there is wisdom. I speak feelingly, for I know how it has been with myself. My feet were just about turning aside, when you showed me the right way, and I thank God that he gave me the courage to walk therein. I shall ever hold you in grateful remembrance as one of my best friends."

XII.

GOLDEN DAYS.

"BRASS, copper, iron; but never gold. Life, like the ages, returns not to golden innocence. It were better, I think, sometimes, that we had not been born."

"I have never thought so."

She who answered thus was a pale, thin woman, who sat by a table sewing. Forty summers and winters had not passed without leaving the marks of scorching sun and traces of frost. But neither summer heats nor winter's cold—not any storm that swept down upon her life—had really marred the beauty of her face. You saw signs of their having touched her; but every sign was in the process of obliteration. Like tempest and drought marks upon the earth, the dews of peace, the gently falling rains, the mild sunshine, were covering them with verdure.

The dress and air of the visitor, who had just spoken, showed her to be a woman in easy circumstances. The two had been close friends in early life ;, but it so happened that their ways in the world had been along diverging paths. Mrs. Wilton had married a "rising man," who soon lifted her into a sphere of fashionable elegance, where, for a long period, she held a kind of queenly sway. Mrs. Grover had been less fortunate in the world's eye. Her husband lacked those qualities by which men rise into high places. But, apart from this, he was a true man in all the better meanings of the phrase; and so far as happiness was concerned, his wife had a larger share than fell to the lot of her friend, Mrs. Wilton. Ease, idleness, luxury was the lot of one; care, labor, and self-denial as to many external things, the lot of the other. After twenty years of divergence, their ways had touched again. The old regard had been quickened into life. Mrs. Wilton found more real satisfaction in an hour's talk with the friend of her youth than in days of intercourse with her fashionable acquaintance, and so came often to the humble residence of Mrs. Grover, now a widow.

On this occasion she had referred, gloomily, to the progression of her life; and spoke with bitterness of her disappointment. Her husband was so absorbed in his business, now grown to a magnitude that taxed every power of his mind, that she said of him—"I have no husband." Children, neglected in earlier years, by the pleasure-loving mother and the business-loving father, had grown up without that moral culture so essential in the formation of character. Nay, worse; had been left to the care of coarse, and often impure-minded servants, for so large a part of their time, that perversions and vitiations had occurred of such a nature visibly affecting their whole after lives. Now, the disappointed mother had little pleasure in them; now, when turning athirst from the world to cisterns where love should have gathered its precious waters, she found them broken into fragments.

"Brass, copper, iron; but never gold. Life,

like the ages, returns not to golden innocence."

Thus, in the bitterness of her disappointment, had she spoken.

"Both the ages and the life may return," answered Mrs. Grover, a light breaking through her pale, translucent face. The *age* will return. Iron, copper, brass, silver, gold. The reverse action was, long ago, commenced. History has marked its progress for eighteen hundred years. If our lives return not, the fault is our own. As for me, I am looking forward to golden days. Already the sky is lifting in the east, and I see faint gleams along the dim horizon."

How strongly were these two women contrasted! The one in plain, poor garments, with the wasting marks of a long over-tasked physical life everywhere to be seen about her person; the other dressed in costly raiment, with hands delicate as an infant's, and no evidence of bodily exhaustion visible. Still stronger was the mental contrast as it stood written in their faces. Years of disappointment had with one been making their silent, almost imperceptible record; while years of patient love and duty, of Christain faith and hope, had left their signs upon the other.

For a little while Mrs. Wilton looked at her old friend with a surprise she did not attempt to conceal. That she was in earnest, the tender thrill in her low voice and the sweet peace that pervaded her countenance were testimonials.

"Golden days in your future? Forgive me, Helen, that I express surprise," said Mrs. Wilton, "but what can one in your situation look forward to in the time to come?"

"As to worldly good?"

"Yes."

"I have children."

A cloud fell over Mrs. Wilton's face.

"Children! She leans on a broken reed who leans on them. I have never had pleasure in children. It has been disappointment from the beginning."

"It has been different with me," replied Mrs. Grover. "I have always had pleasure in my children. The sweetest days of my life were those spent with my babies in my arms. They were very close to heaven. In the golden years of their infantile innocence, angels were near them, and my soul had a blessed perception of their presence. I had care, and work, and self-denial; but the compensation was above all. Home was my garden, and these children were my choice flowers. With what untiring solicitude did I watch over them. Every weed that pushed its leaves above the soil I plucked out by the roots. Every vile worm, or destructive insect, that fastened on leaf or stem, I removed. I kept the ground loose, that dew, sunshine and air might go down to the roots and give them an ever increasing vitality; and I trained the branches into such beauty of form as my skill and their peculiarities would admit. There was little time for ease, for pleasure, for self-indulgence. I could not eat the bread of idleness. I often got weary over my never-ending task. But this assurance was in my heart: 'Train up a child in the way he should go, and when he is old he will not depart from it.' My faith was unquestioning. I had peace and hope here, my friend."

And Mrs. Grover laid her hand upon her breast.

"And what of your children now?" asked Mrs. Wilton.

"Two are with their father in heaven—safe, happy. My youngest, whom you have seen—a dear, loving, thoughtful little girl—is at school. And here is a letter from my oldest son, now in a Western city, whither he went, two years ago, at the solicitation of a merchant who had taken a fancy to him."

Mrs. Grover took from a drawer in her work-table a letter and read:

"DEAREST MOTHER:—Every thing is going right with me. Mr. L—— is one of the best of men, and I am doing all in my power to give him satisfaction. I could not deny myself the pleasure of reading to him a few sentences from your last letter, where you speak so beautifully on the subject of doing right, under all circumstances, for the sake of right, and not for the sake of pleasing or gaining worldly gain. He did not say any thing, but I could see by the expression of his face that he was pleased. On the day after he said to me, 'Frank, has your mother an income?' I could only tell him the truth. He looked serious for a little while. Then he asked how much of my salary I remitted you; and when I answered that I sent all except one hundred dollars on which I clothed myself, he took my hand and said: 'Frank, that is the best thing I have heard of you. You are a good boy, and will never be the loser by any thing done for your mother.' I felt very proud, mother. Praise is good sometimes.

"Well, on the next day Mr. L—— said to me: 'Frank, has your mother any particular reason for remaining at the East?' And when I answered, 'None that I know of,' he said, 'Write to her, and convey my earnest solicitation to remove to this place. Tell her that I have two or three pleasant little houses, of which she can make her choice; and that, on the day she arrives, I will double your salary, so that there can remain no question as to the ways and means of living in comfort.' Wasn't that good? Wasn't that noble? Don't you wonder how I could keep this good news back from the first sentence in my letter? It was hard work. But I wanted to lead you on, dear mother, and not make the surprise too sudden.

"Of course you will come! There is nothing to keep you in P——. When shall I expect you and dear Fanny? I shall hardly know her—you say she has grown so much. Oh, won't we be all so happy together? You shall live an easier life here than you have ever lived. With my salary doubled, there will be no more hard work for you. The golden days are coming, mother! Write immediately. I shall be all impatience until I get your letter. Your loving son, FRANK."

Mrs. Grover's voice had faltered several times as she read this letter, and as she lifted her eyes on closing it to the face of her friend, they were full of tears—glad tears, in which love's sunshine made rainbows.

"So you see that my golden days are coming," she said.

Mrs. Wilton dropped her gaze to the floor, and sighed heavily. For her no golden days like these were coming. While idle, neglectful and asleep, an enemy had sowed tares in her field, and now she was in the harvest time of bitter regrets and disappointments. In the pure mirror of her friend's life, she saw reflected the errors, the criminal neglect, the poor self-seeking and vanity of her own; and she went away in sadness and self-condemnation. But the truth which had come to her came too late. The evil had been done. For her, as she had well said, there were no golden days in store, to make beautiful the last period of her life on earth. As she had sown, so she must reap. To each comes his own harvest.

XIII.

THE COMPANY WE KEEP.

"We know people by the company they keep."

The tone of voice, rather than the remark, caused me to turn and look at the speaker. She was a handsomely dressed woman, with a fresh, attractive face, and that easy self-conscious air which we see in persons who are altogether satisfied as to their social standing and personal merit. To be frank, I did not like the expression of her countenance.

"Yes, birds of a feather flock together," tritely answered the one to whom she had addressed her remark.

"For my part," said the first lady—let me call her, for convenience of reference, Mrs. Grandlea—"I am particularly guarded in this thing. I must be certain as to who is who before I admit any one into even a recognizable acquaintanceship. We can't be too particular here. I know how it is with me; I judge others by their associates, and expect similar judgment in return."

"We may be deceived sometimes," remarked the other lady. "We can't always tell who is who."

"I find no difficulty," said Mrs. Grandlea. "There are social landmarks always in sight, if we will but heed them; and, in a country like this, where the lower classes are forever trying to thrust themselves in amongst us, we must observe these landmarks if we would keep ourselves away from contact with the common and unclean."

Now, it so happened that I knew a great deal more of Mrs. Grandlea's ancestry than she did herself. I very well remembered her father when he kept a small grocery and tea store in Baltimore, and her mother when she did good service to customers behind the counter of this same store. They were honest, good people, and respected by every one, but, according to Mrs. Grandlea's present ideas of things, among the common and unclean.

"I have my own trials," continued Mrs. Grandlea. "I have to be almost rude sometimes. But I will make others keep their places. So far, and no farther—that is my law. Only yesterday, in getting into a street car, I found myself alongside of one of Evans's store girls,—Mary L——, they call her."

"Oh, yes; I know who you mean," was replied.

"A pleasant enough person in the store," continued Mrs. Grandlea; "always polite and obliging—always good-natured, and quite intelligent, by the way. But that doesn't help the matter any. She belongs to one class in society and I to another. Well, as I was saying, I found myself alongside of Mary L——. She turned and looked at me, with a smile and a nod quite as easy and self-possessed as the first lady in the land. Oh, but I was angry. I scarcely think she will provoke another such a look as I gave her. The assurance of this class of people is terrible."

Now, it so happened that I also knew as much about the antecedents of Mary L—— as I did about those of Mrs. Grandlea. Her father, who has been dead for some years, was a man of high culture and great moral worth. Few citizens of his day stood so well in public estimation; and there was no social circle but would have felt his presence as an honor or an ornament. Mrs. L—— was as fine in quality as her husband, and as much beloved and respected. In a time of public disaster, when fortunes were being wrecked on a stormy sea, Mr. L—— died. Rich to-day, his family was poor to-morrow. Mary was fifteen years old then. Her mother, living on a small remnant of property, saved from the flood of misfortune, was able to keep her and her younger sister at school for two or three years. Then, her means being exhausted, she attempted that poorest, and hardest, and usually most deceptive expedient of widows—the establishment of a genteel boarding-house.

Two years a slave, death wrought out for Mrs. L—— a violent emancipation. Her furniture, or the chief part at least, was sold for rent, and the discouraged and almost heart-broken mother retired to a couple of cheap rooms with her two daughters. It was then that Mary L—— awoke fairly to her duties and responsibilities. Love for her mother made her strong and brave. "It is our time now," she said to her sister, and the sister was ready to respond. Mary was just twenty years of age; the sister eighteen. "What shall we do?" was the question to be decided. The providence by which we are all led guided their feet. The way that first opened to them they accepted. Both became saleswomen in dry-goods stores, at first receiving each but three dollars a week. For five years they have illustrated that noble truth so tersely expressed by Pope:

> "Honor and shame from no condition rise;
> Act well your part, there all the honor lies."

Their mother has every comfort their loving hearts and busy hands are able to provide.

The ladies dropped their voices, and I

heard no more of their conversation. A few weeks afterwards, in talking with a friend who was well acquainted with Mrs. Grandlea, I spoke of her shallow pretensions and blind self-conceit—referring particularly to her un-lady-like treatment of Mary L——.

"Oh, as to that," was my friend's answer, "Mary L—— is in every way her superior, and keeps a great deal better company."

"I shouldn't wonder," said I.

"I know it," she responded. "There is Mrs. M——, one of Mrs. Grandlea's very intimate friends. You may see them on the street together any fair day. Now Mrs. M—— is a weak, vain, impure woman. She cannot talk about any thing but persons—the way they dress, look, act, and live. Of principles that lie at the base of action; of just moral sentiments; of womanly duty—she knows little, and cares less. But she is rich, keeps her carriage, gives handsome entertainments, and moves in 'good society.'

"But," she continued, "this woman alone is not taken to her bosom. If we are very intimate with a person we must associate with their friends also."

"Does that follow?" I asked.

"It follows in the sense I mean," was answered. "Our closest companions—our dearest friends—are our feelings and thoughts. We dwell with them continually. They are the cherished ones of our household, with whom we enjoy daily communion. Whoever takes us into near association must take them also. Mrs. Grandlea, under this view of the case, which I hold to be correct, keeps very bad company when she keeps that of Mrs. M——. Her associates, in this connection, are essentially common and unclean. Mary L—— would turn from them in disgust. Moreover, I fear that much cannot be said in favor of her own interior friends—the spiritual companions that are in harmony with her inner life—if we are to form any true judgment of a person from words and actions. I never heard her admire the beauty of goodness in any one; I have never heard her express a noble sentiment; I have never known her to separate action from personality. But I have heard from her lips the utterance of sentiments that were a shame to humanity—full of pride, envy, ill-will, hatred, malice, covetousness.

"And now," added my friend—"let me mention an incident exactly in point. I did not see its full force until this moment. Mrs. Grandlea honored me one day last week with a formal call, which, after she had retired, I made up my mind not to return, and so close with her our visiting acquaintance. I don't know any words that so clearly express what I felt in her presence as those she used when speaking of Mary L——, 'common and unclean.' Scandalous social gossip; mean detraction of others; cant and vulgarity—these made up the burden of her talk. I was shocked, annoyed, disturbed; and when she withdrew, I made up my mind that she stood too far below me to warrant any social intimacy. Before she came, my mind was tranquil. I was busy in thought with good purposes. After she went away, I found it impossible to draw back the pure and pleasant companions with whom, in my spirit, I had been taking sweet counsel. You may smile at my weak impressibility. But it is just so."

"There are few of us," I replied, "who are not equally impressible, as we would discover by noting carefully our varying states. Each person we meet affects us differently from another person. One elevates, and another depresses our feelings. One reveals to us moral beauty, and another hurts our eyes with deformity."

"As I was saying," went on the lady, "I found myself unable to draw back the pure and pleasant companions with whom I had been taking sweet counsel. So, believing that a change would help my uncomfortable state of mind, I put on my things, and went out to do some shopping. You may think it a fancy; but I know that it was a reality—when I sat down at one of the counters in Evans's store, and looked up into Mary L——'s bright, pure, refined countenance, the evil companions with whom Mrs. Grandlea's visit had cursed me went out of my heart, like departing shadows, when the morning breaks. No, it was not fancy. Her voice, as it fell upon my ears, struck the chord of truer harmonies. It seemed as if I almost heard the words—'Peace, be still.' There were not many customers in the store, and taking advantage of this, I had ten minutes' talk with Miss L——, as I looked over the goods I wished to purchase. What a different impression from that of Mrs. Grandlea did she make upon me! The instincts and culture of a true lady were visible in every tone and sentence. There was nothing obtrusive; as I drew her out, she spoke, uttering sentiments that did honor to her sex and human nature.

"I could not help saying to her, as I rose to leave—'Mary, you and I should know each other better.' A slight increase of color, as if her heart were beating quicker, warmed up her face. But she made no reply. Whether she were thinking of the social distinctions that barred her from a free entrance into the circle where I move; or whether she were not willing to come into any closer relation to me, I cannot tell. All I know is, that she did not respond as it was in my heart to have her."

"She is particular as to the company she keeps," I said, smiling.

"Yes, and for that I give her all honor," was the smiling answer, "even if she draws back at my invitation."

"Taking your view of the case," I said, "some of our 'best' people keep very bad company."

"They do, unquestionably; and this will continue to be so until some other indorsement than 'Money' is required on the passport that admits you into 'good society.' Human nature is the same in all social grades. Meanness, vice, poverty of intellect, moral inversions and crimes are limited to no class. You meet them in the aristocrat's gilded drawing-rooms as often as in the poor artisan's humble dwelling. Bad company is to be found everywhere; and if we would avoid its demoralizing influence, we must take our associates from the pure and good, no matter in which sphere of life they may happen to move."

XIV.

DIGGING UP SEEDS.

"THEY'LL never come up!" said the voice of a child. It was fretful and impatient. "They've been planted three days. I knew thoy wouldn't grow."

The little boy who thus complained was standing over a bed in the garden, where he had some flower-seeds. He had been there two or three times every day since the seeds were planted, hoping to see their first green shoots piercing the earth. Impatience could wait no longer. And now he commenced digging down to see if the seed had sprouted. Two or three were turned up, each with the small white germ breaking through the horny covering. Ho tried to put them back; but, in doing so, broke off the tender germs.

"What are you doing?" cried the child's mother, who came down one of the garden walks just at this time, and saw him uncovering the seeds which she had instructed him how to sow. There was a tone of anger in her voice. The child started; then frowned and pouted his lips.

"I knew they wouldn't come up," he said.

"What are you doing?" The mother repeated her question sharply. Then seeing what had been done, she let angry feelings have vent.

"You're a naughty, impatient child!" she exclaimed; "seeds don't come up in a night! Why couldn't you wait? Just see what you've done! There!—that seed has sprouted; and now it's good for nothing. You've ruined your garden! You're the silliest child I ever knew, and I am out of all patience with you."

What answer did the child make?

"I don't care!" and he ran on to the flower-bed, and trampled it with his feet. Blind passion was, for the time, his master.

The mother, stronger, but scarcely wiser than her child, caught him by the arm and almost dragged him into the house.

"You naughty, naughty boy," she said, "I'll punish you for this." And she put him into a room by himself, telling him that he should stay there alone until evening.

A friend, walking in the garden at the time, saw what passed between the child and his mother.

"Unwise, unwise," she said to herself. "What an opportunity for a lesson that her boy might never have forgotten!—but failing to improve the occasion, she has hurt instead of teaching him."

Soon after, the boy's mother and her friend were sitting together.

"Where is Harry?" asked the latter.

"I've sent him to his room," replied the mother.

"As a punishment?"

"Yes."

"What has he been doing?"

"Giving way to that passionate temper, which will, if not restrained, bring him one day into serious trouble." And then she related the incident about the flower-seeds.

"We do not become very much wiser as we grow older," remarked the friend; "only our imperfect hands dig up the seed of higher things before they have time to germinate."

"I can remember," answered the mother, half-smiling, half-serious, "doing the same thing when a child—digging up seed I had planted, to see if they were beginning to grow. I ought not to be severe with Harry; but then his impatient spirit must be checked, or it will rule him to his injury when he becomes a man. It was not because he dug up the seed, but because he trampled on his flower-bed, that I punished him."

"And are you wiser now than when you were a child?" asked the friend. "Are you not doing the same things to-day, only in a higher region of life?"

"What?"

"Digging up the good seeds you have planted in your child,-and impatiently trampling on the flower-beds of his soul."

"Is this so? Are you in earnest?" The mother's face grew very serious.

"May I talk plainly? Won't you be hurt, or offended?"

"With you I can never be offended. I know your heart," said the mother.

"I have been with you for a month."

"And a pleasant month it has been, my friend—pleasant and also profitable. You have helped me to perceive many things not perceived by my dull eyes before. You have strengthened my weak hands; you have confirmed my failing purposes. Your visit has done me good. And now, say on."

"How many times, in that month, have I seen you repeat the incident of to-day?"

"What incident?"

"That of digging down impatiently into your child's mind, to see if the seeds you had planted were beginning to sprout."

"Have I been so blind?" she asked.

"So it has seemed to me."

"Will you come down to particulars? Then I can understand you better. Don't be afraid of hurting me. I love my boy. I wish to be a true mother. I feel, more deeply than

I can express, my inability to guide him aright. He is wayward, impatient, and passionate; and do which I will, I fail to weaken these dangerous tendencies of his soul."

"It is because you do not see clearly. Unless there be a clear sight, how can there be a sure hand?"

"Help me to a clearer sight, my friend," said the mother. "Lift the scales from my eyes. Show me the true way."

"I read to-day in this book," answered the friend, lifting a small volume entitled, 'Thoughts in My Garden,' "a passage that seems as if written just for your case. Will you have it?"

"O, yes. I am searching for light." And the friend read:

"When a child begins gardening, he is so impatient to see the result of his work, that he is almost sure to dig up his seeds in order to find if they are sprouting. The parent looks on and perhaps smiles complacently at the child's folly, bidding him be patient for a few days till the little plants have time to show themselves. Yet it is quite probable that that very parent treats the seeds of thought he sows in the mind of the child with an impatience just as foolish as that of the child over his flower-seeds. He tells him a truth, and expects it to spring up and bear fruit as soon as it is sown. He looks to reap the harvest in the character of his child before the seed-time is over. He probes his child's heart with questions to find out if the truth he sows is germinating, before the warmth of the Divine love has had opportunity to expand the germ and quicken it into life. He will not wait for the gradual way in which Divine Providence, through the ministry of circumstance, quickens the spiritual nature of the child; and then by the rain of His truth and the sunshine of His love causes the seeds sown, it may be, years before, and lying till then darkly and inert, to take root and grow, and bear fruit many fold."

"There is a time to plant," said the friend, as she closed the book; "a time in which the seed must lie passive in the earth, hidden from sight, while germination takes place; a time for the spring blade—for the opening flower—for the ripening fruit and grain. For all the processes we must wait. If we look for the shooting blade before the period of germination is over, we shall be disappointed—if for ripe fruit in the spring time of growth and development, our disappointment will be none the less sure."

The mother did not answer; but sat, with eyes cast down, lost in thought. A veil had dropped from her eyes, and now she saw things clearly that were hidden before; saw how, in her ignorance and impatience, she had been perpetually disturbing the earth of her child's mind, and hindering the growth of the good seeds she had planted there. After a few moments, she got up and left the room, without speaking. Shutting the door after her, as she went out, she ran quickly to the chamber in which she had shut up her boy, and went in upon him so suddenly, that he had no warning of her approach. She found him sitting on the floor, amid the contents of a toilette case, which she had received only a week before as a birth-day gift from her husband. Scent bottles, sackets, perfumed soaps, hand mirrors, and all the elegant etceteras of a lady's dressing-box, lay in disorder around.

A pulse of anger sent the blood leaping along the mother's veins ; her eyes flashed an indignant light ; fierce words were on her lips ; her hands shut in a convulsive grip. The child looked up with a frightened aspect. What a moment of trial and peril ! In the pause, a voice seemed to say, "Beware !"

"What is Harry doing ?" she asked, in a tone of gentle inquiry, as she sat down on the floor beside her child, and looked on him with motherly tenderness in her eyes. Wonder took the place of fear in the child's countenance.

"I'll put them all back again," he said, in a penitent voice, turning to the articles scattered around him on the floor, and commencing to gather them up. "There isn't any thing broken, mamma."

The mother had to restrain herself. She would have stayed the child's hand. But, by help of the new light that had streamed into her mind, she saw that in doing so there was danger of hurting something of far more value than a perfumed bottle, or a mirror not two inches in diameter. He had committed an error that he was anxious to repair. He was trying to put himself right with his mother by undoing a wrong.

"I was a naughty boy, and I'm so sorry," he said, pausing to look up at his mother, and read her state of feeling in her eyes.

"It was my birth-day present," answered the mother. "Father gave it to me." Her tones were serious, but not rebuking. "I should have been so grieved if any thing had been broken."

"But there isn't any thing broken, mamma —not the least bit of a thing. Oh!" An ejaculation of pain closed the sentence, as a small Bohemian glass bottle dropped from his hands and broke into fragments. His face grew instantly pale—his lips quivered—he lifted his eyes with a pleading look of fear and suffering. The mother had to guard herself. She, as well as her boy, was passing through discipline.

"Oh, mamma," cried out the child, in the overpowering grief of his little heart; and he hid his face among her garments and sobbed wildly. The mother's heart had become very tender during the progress of this scene. How could she help putting her arms around her grieving boy and weeping with him and comforting him?

"Don't cry about it, darling," she said, with her lips against his cheeks. "You didn't mean to do it; and I can buy another bottle. If you won't touch my toilette case again——"

"Oh, I'll never, never touch it again!" he answered, eagerly. "I'm so sorry! And I'm sorry I dug up the seeds, mamma. It seemed so long. And I was sure they'd never come up. Oh, mamma! if you hadn't scolded me—if you'd said, as Miss Wilson did yesterday, 'Wait just a little longer, Harry, and you'll see them shooting up,' I wouldn't have been so naughty.'

15

The mother caught her breath and swallowed two or three times; then laid her hot cheek down among the golden curls of her boy, and held him tightly against her heart.

"Only be patient," said her friend, as they sat together not long afterward. "The ground of a child's mind is good ground. If you fill it with good seeds and let them lie there undisturbed by impatience or passion, they will surely germinate and grow. It is not because the ground is bad, but because it is so often dug over and trampled upon, that so little of greenness—so little of bud blossom—appear in the lives of children. Some seeds take the quickening impulse of nature in a few days, while others lie in the ground as if there were no centre of vitality in them for months. The wise gardener takes note of this difference, and waits the appointed time with unwavering confidence. We should be as wise as he in our human gardens; nay, wiser, for the flowers that bloom and the fruits that grow in them are far more precious."

XV.

THE SHADOWS WE CAST.

A CHILD was playing with some building blocks; and, as the mimic castle rose before his eyes in graceful proportions, a new pleasure swelled in his heart. He felt himself to be the creator of a "thing of beauty," and was conscious of a new-born power. Arch, wall, buttress, gateway, draw-bridge, lofty tower, and battlement were all the work of his hands. He was in wonder at his own skill in thus creating, from an unseemly pile of blocks, a structure of such rare design.

Silently he stood and gazed upon his castle with something of the pride of an architect, who sees, after months or years of skilfully applied labor, some grand conception in his art, embodied in imperishable stone. Then he moved around, viewing it on every side. It did not seem to him a toy, reaching only a few inches in height, and covering but a square foot of ground, but a real castle, lifting itself hundreds of feet upward towards the blue sky, and spreading wide upon the earth its ample foundations. As the idea grew more and more perfect, his strange pleasure increased. Now he stood, with folded arms, wrapped in the overmastering illusion—now walked slowly around, viewing the structure on all sides, and noting every minute particular—and now sat down, and bent over it with the fondness of a mother bending over her child. Again he arose, purposing to obtain another and more distant view of his work. But his foot struck against one of the buttresses, and instantly, with a crash, wall, tower, and battlement fell in hopeless ruin.

In the room, with the boy, sat his father, reading. The crash disturbed him; and he uttered a sharp, angry rebuke, glancing, for a moment, towards the startled child, and then returning his eyes to the attractive page before him, unconscious of the shadow he had cast upon the heart of his child. Tears came into those fair blue orbs, dancing in light a moment before. From the frowning face of his father, to which his glance was suddenly turned, the child looked back to the shapeless ruins of his castle. Is it any wonder that he bowed his face in silence upon them, and wet them with his tears.

For more than five minutes, he sat as still as if sleeping; then in a mournful kind of way, yet almost noiselessly, he commenced restoring to the box, from which he had taken them, the many-shaped pieces that, fitly joined together, had grown into a noble building. After the box was filled, he replaced the cover, and laid it carefully upon a shelf in the closet.

Poor child! That shadow was a deep one, and long in passing away. His mother found him, half an hour afterwards, asleep on the floor, with cheeks flushed to an unusual brightness. She knew nothing of that troubled passage in his young life; and the father had forgotten, in the attractions of the book he read, the momentary annoyance expressed in words and tones, with a power in them to shadow the heart of his child.

A young wife had busied herself for many days in preparing a pleasant surprise for her husband. The work was finished at last; and now she awaited his return with a heart full of warm emotions. A dressing-gown, and a pair of elegantly embroidered slippers, wrought by her own skilful fingers, were the gifts which she meant to delight him. What a troop of pleasant fancies was in her heart! How, almost impatiently, did she wait for the coming twilight, which was to be dawn, not approaching darkness to her!

At last, she heard the step of her husband in the passage, and her pulses leaped with fluttering delight. Like a bird upon the wing, she almost flew down to meet him, impatient for the kiss that awaited her.

To men in the world of business, few days pass without their disappointments and perplexities. It is men's business to bear this in a manly spirit. They form but a portion of life's discipline, and should make them stronger, braver, and more enduring. Unwisely, and we may say unjustly, too many men fail to leave their business cares and troubles in their stores, workshops, or counting-rooms, at the day's decline. They wrap them in bundles, and carry them home to shadow their households.

It was so with the young husband on this particular occasion. The stream of business had taken an eddying whirl, and thrown his vessel backwards, instead of onwards, for a brief space; and, though it was still in the current, and gliding safely onward again, the jar and disappointment had fretted his mind severely. There was no heart-warmth in the kiss he gave his wife, not because love had failed in any degree, but because he had let care overshadow love. He drew his arm around her; but she was conscious of a diminished pressure in that embracing arm.

"Are you not well?"

With what tender concern was the question asked!

"Very well." He might be in body, but not in mind; that was plain; for his voice was far from being cheerful.

She played and sang his favorite pieces, hoping to restore, by the charm of music, brightness to his spirit. But she was conscious of only partial success. There was still a gravity in his manner never perceived before. At tea-time, she smiled upon him so sweetly across the table, and talked to him on such attractive themes, that the right expression returned to his countenance; and he looked as happy as she could desire.

From the tea-table, they returned to their pleasant parlor. And now the time had come for offering her gift, and receiving the coveted reward of glad surprise, followed by sweet kisses and loving words. Was she selfish? Did she think more of her reward than of the pleasure she would bestow? But that is questioning too closely.

"I will be back in a moment," she said,

and, passing from the room, she went lightly up the stairs. Both tone and manner betrayed her secret, or rather the possession of a secret with which her husband was to be surprised. Scarcely had her loving face faded from before his eyes, when thought returned, with a single bound, to an unpleasant event of the day; and the waters of his spirit were again troubled. He had actually arisen, and crossed the floor once or twice, moved by a restless concern, when his wife came back with the dressing-gown and slippers. She was trying to force her countenance into a grave expression, to hold back the smiles that were continually striving to break in truant circles around her lips, when a single glance at her husband's face told her that the spirit, driven away by the exorcism of her love, had returned again to his bosom. He looked at her soberly, as she came forward.

"What are these?" he asked, almost coldly, repressing surprise, and affecting an ignorance, in regard to the beautiful present she held in her hands, that he did not feel.

"They are for you, dear. I made them."

"For me! Nonsense! What do I want with such jimcrackery? This is a woman's wear. Do you think I would disfigure my feet with embroidered slippers, or dress up in a calico gown? Put them away, dear. Your husband is too much of a man to robe himself in gay colors, like a clown or an actor." And he waved his hand with an air of contempt. There was a cold, sneering manner about him, partly affected and partly real—the real born of his uncomfortable state of mind. Yet he loved his sweet wife, and would not, of set purpose, have wounded her for the world.

This unexpected repulse—this cruel reception of her present, over which she had wrought, patiently, in golden hope, for many days—this dashing to the earth of her brimful cup of joy, just as it touched her lips, was more than the fond young wife could bear. To hide the tears that came rushing to her eyes, she turned away from her husband; and to conceal the sobs she had no power to repress, she went almost hurriedly from the room; and, going back to the chamber from whence she had brought the present, she laid it away out of sight in a closet. Then covering her face with her hands, she sat down, and strove with herself to be calm. But the shadow was too deep—the heartache too heavy.

In a little while, her husband followed her, and discovering, something to his surprise, that she was weeping, said, in a slightly reproving voice:

"Why, bless me! not in tears! What a silly little puss you are! Why didn't you tell me you thought of making a dressing-gown and pair of slippers, and I would have vetoed the matter at once? You couldn't hire me to wear such flaunting things. Come back to the parlor"—he took hold of her arm and lifted her from the chair—"and sing and play for me. 'The Dream Waltz,' or 'The Tremolo,' 'Dearest May,' or 'The Stilly Night,' are worth more to me than forty dressing-gowns or a cargo of embroidered slippers."

Almost by force, he led her back to the

parlor, and placed her on the music-stool. He selected a favorite piece, and laid it before her. But tears were in her eyes; and she could not see a note. Over the keys her fingers passed in skilful touches; but, when she tried to take up the song, utterance failed; and sobs broke forth instead of words.

"How foolish!" said the husband, in a vexed tone. "I'm surprised at you!" And he turned from the piano, and walked across the room.

A little while the sad young wife remained where she was left thus alone, and in partial anger. Then, rising, she went slowly from the room—her husband not seeking to restrain her—and, going back to her chamber, sat down in darkness.

The shadow which had been cast upon her spirit was very deep; and, though the hidden sun came out again right early, it was a long time before his beams had power to scatter the clouds that floated in love's horizon.

The shadows we cast! Father, husband, wife, sister, brother, son, neighbor—are we not all casting shadows daily, on some hearts that are pining for the sunlight of our faces? We have given you two pictures of life, true pictures, not as a mirror, but as a kaleidoscope. In all their infinitely varied relations, men and women, selfishly or thoughtlessly—from design, weakness, or ignorance—are casting their shadows upon hearts that are pining for sunlight. A word, a look, a tone, an act will cast a shadow, and sadden a spirit for hours and days. Speak kindly, act kindly, be forgetters of self, and regarders of others, and you will cast but few shadows along the path of life. The true gentleman is always tender of the feelings of others—always watchful, lest he wound unintentionally—always thinking, when with others, of their pleasure instead of his own. He casts but few shadows. Be gentlemen—ladies, or—in a word that includes all graces and excellencies—Christians; for it is the Christian who casts fewest shadows of all.

IV.

A LITTLE MORE SUNSHINE.

"PERVERSE and desperately wicked," said Mr. Nolan, speaking with the emphasis of a man who feels the wretched import of his words. "By nature, the heart is corrupt, depraved, godless. More and more clearly does this become apparent every day."

The conversation had turned upon children, with half a dozen of which Mr. Nolan was blessed or cursed, he hardly knew which; and this sentence was but the utterance of an increased conviction, from experience, of the truth expressed.

"Not so apparent in children as in men and women," answered the friend with whom Mr. Nolan was talking.

"There I must differ with you," was the prompt reply. "The fountain is impure at the source."

"Not in the sense your language implies," returned the friend; "not in its full meaning. Children are born in innocence. The evil in them is only latent, and becomes developed through favoring circumstances. The proclivity exists, nothing more; and like a germ in the seed, will, as external things conspire, start into life. We will compare them to a garden of rich ground, in which lie thistle seeds and the seeds of all manner of vile and poisonous plants. This ground will nourish good seed if they be planted, and produce good fruit in abundance. God has made it our duty to plant these good seeds, and to nurture the tender shoots that first spring up. This is even more essential than the repression and weeding out of evil plants, to which most parents solely confine themselves. The good seed may drop in as it will—the good plants grow and thrive as best they can. The parent finds more congenial work, if I may venture the assertion, in striking down and rooting out evil, than in cultivating what is good. Most people, I fear, have no faith in good, and therefore do not attempt its growth and culture. Evil is something about which they are better instructed, and they have, besides, more faith in force than in development."

A little boy entered, crossing the floor to his father with noisy feet. He had come to ask a favor, and his desire controlling his mind, he had not thought about the manner of his entrance into the room; and so he was really innocent of any purpose to give offence. But he did give offence. His tramping and scuffling—yea, his very presence at the moment—disturbed his father. Mr. Nolan hushed the request, trembling on his lips, with a frown. The boy, in his eagerness, was not to be repressed. He crowded up to his father, who tried to hold him at a distance, and threw in, impetuously, his questions. The answer was—"No—no—I tell you no!" There was no light of kindness in the face of Mr. Nolan. His voice was hard. His manner repellant. The boy went sulking away, managing, ere he left the room, to knock over a chair. Then followed a contest between him and his father about lifting the chair and restoring it to its place. Mr. Nolan was triumphant through brute force.

The conversation went on again, but was soon interrupted by the appearance of another child, who was frowned upon and refused as the first had been. Leading this one to the door of the apartment, Mr. Nolan pushed her out, and calling to his wife, said, in no very amiable tone of voice:

"Mrs. Nolan, I wish you would look to it that these children don't leave the nursery. I can't be interrupted in this way."

"You see how it is," remarked Mr. Nolan, as he shut the door and came back to his friend. The friend said nothing. There was a pause, slightly embarrassing to both

"You see how it is," resumed Mr. Nolan; "there is no respect, nor order, no spontaneous obedience in them. It is so, according to my observation, with all children. As to what you said just now about ground and seed, and garden culture, it is all a nice thing to talk and write about. It looks well in sermons and books; but, practically, it assumes another aspect."

Mr. Nolan did not speak like a man who was altogether satisfied as to what he was saying. In fact, he was only trying to excuse himself to himself, for the truth, as presented by his friend, touched his inner convictions. There stood on a table, near a window, the shade of which had been drawn down, three or four pots of choice flowers. As Mr. Nolan finished his last sentence, his eyes happened to fall upon these plants. They afforded the means of changing a subject that had grown unpleasant. Rising, he went to the window and drew up the blind, and as he did so the warm sunshine came in upon the flowers.

"It is so strange," he remarked, "that some people never appear to think that flowers must have the sunshine. No one in this house cares for flowers except myself, and you don't know the trouble I have to keep them fresh and vigorous. Mrs. Nolan says that I mustn't depend on her, she has as much as she can do to see after her human flowers." Mr. Nolan gave a forced laugh that did not sound musical. "As for servants," he continued, "they are of no account here. Whatever they do is sure to be the worst thing possible. Now, you would suppose that a grown-up woman, going through a room like this and putting it in order, would, at the very first movement, pull up the blind and let in the sunshine upon these flowers. You would suppose that, seeing the earth dry and hard about the roots, she would supply them with water. But nothing of the kind happens. They might starve and die for all my servant cares."

Mr. Nolan rang a bell and ordered a watering-pot of water, that he might sprinkle the flowers himself. As the thirsty earth about the roots drank up the grateful supply, and the leaves shook and nodded, and quivered with delight as the rain fell over them, flashing back the sunbeams from every drop, he said, touching with his fingers a half-opened bud:

"Isn't that exquisite? This is a new

French rose. I bought it in New York last fall, and have been nursing it with the greatest solicitude. It is very delicate, and on that account very rare."

"Suppose," said the friend, "you were to remove it to a place where it would get no sunshine. Would it grow strong and symmetrical? Would it bear fragrant and beautiful flowers?"

"What a question!" Mr. Nolan did not conceal his surprise. "Of course it would not."

"It would still live," remarked the friend.

"Probably; all organic forms are tenacious of life in their degree."

"But grow out of its natural symmetry."

"Yes, and become stunted and unsightly."

"Suppose," said the friend, "that, after suffering through a period of time for lack of sunshine, until it was dwarfed and deformed in growth, you should bring it back into warm golden light again; what would follow?"

"Its life would respond to the sunlight. A

new impulse would pervade its whole substance, from root to leaf. A little while, and you would see new buds starting. There would be a fresher greenness and signs of coming beauty."

Mr. Nolan spoke with rising enthusiasm. He loved flowers, and all that concerned them interested him.

His friend laid a hand impressively on his arm and said:

"You have other flowers in this house."

A slight shadow fell over Mr. Nolan's face, as he turned and looked at his friend.

"You spoke of them just now in referring to your wife."

"What flowers!"

"Have you forgotten? Human flowers. They are yours as well as Mrs. Nolan's."

"Human flowers!" Mr. Nolan was brought back to new thought so suddenly, that he was slightly bewildered.

"They must have sunshine, or they will grow up dwarfed and unsightly. Pardon the plain speech of a true friend, when he says that, so far as his observation goes, you do not raise the blinds of your heart, and let in the sunbeams upon your home garden. Two of your children came in just now, with natural and innocent requests. You did not smile upon them. I saw the light go out of your face as they opened the door. Can love grow in their hearts, and blossom with sweetness in their lives under shadow and frown? No more than your cherished flower there, deprived of the sunbeams. Ah, my friend, you must give these children of yours a little more sunshine."

The friend paused. He was not certain as to the effect of this free speech, which had been almost extorted from him under the pressure of what he had witnessed.

Mr. Nolan dropped his eyes to the floor and stood very still. He was not offended, but startled into conviction. Truth had flashed into his mind, and given it a sudden revelation. As he thus stood, the door of the room opened again, and the boy who had been driven away a little while before, thrust himself forward. There was in his manner a kind of dogged resolution. He was, evidently, prepared for frowns and denial; and determined, in face of these, to battle bravely for his ends, and gain them if possible. A human flower, not often in the sunshine, there was, as he then appeared, but little of beauty and sweetness about him. He closed the door with a loud *bang* that jarred the father's nerves, and cut frowning lines into his forehead.

"A little sunshine," whispered his friend, and the harsh lines were smoothed out.

"What does my son want?" There was kindness and fatherly interest in Mr. Nolan's voice.

A quick change passed over the boy. The unpleasant hardness went out of his face, and a soft, child-like beauty pervaded every feature. The headlong abruptness with which he had entered the room gave place to a restrained quiet of demeanor, and approaching his father in a respectful way, he caught one of his hands, and looking up at him, said, in coaxing tones:

"Won't you give me two sheets of paper and a pencil, and won't you just make me a little book, so that I can draw pictures?"

Two impulses struggled for a little while in the mind of Mr. Nolan. The better impulse was victorious. He went to his secretary, and taking out two sheets of paper, folded them as desired.

"Is that right?" he asked, looking with a smile upon his boy.

"O, yes, indeed, papa! Just what I wanted. It's so kind in you! Now, can't I have a pencil?"

"Certainly," and Mr. Nolan gave him a pencil.

"O, thank you!" and the child put up his mouth for a kiss. A few minutes had wrought in him a wonderful transformation. Then he went singing from the room.

"There is a wonderful power in sunshine," said the friend, when they were alone again. "It fills the earth with beauty and fragrance; it gives grain to our fields and fruit to our orchards. And it is as essential to our homes as to the earth. Human plants can no more live and grow into lovely forms without it, than a flower or a tree. But I will not seek by words to enforce the lesson. Your own eyes have seen and your own heart felt the truth of what I affirm. Dear friend! open the windows and let in the sunshine. You cannot give these olive-plants too freely of its health-giving influence. Pour it down upon them, and they will make beautiful and fragrant, loving and delightful, the home that, you will forgive me for saying, has not always dwelt under a cloudless sky."